A Very Crafty Christmas
A Misty Vale Cozy Mystery
Book 1
Sarah Lewin © 2025

A Very Crafty Christmas
Book #1 Misty Vale Cosy Mystery
This is a work of fiction. Names, characters, places, and incidents either are the product of the author's imagination or are used fictitiously. Any resemblance to actual persons, living or dead, events, or locales is entirely coincidental.

First edition April 2025
ISBN 978-1-7637430-6-9 (ebook)
ISBN 978-1-7637430-3-8 (Paperback)
www.sarahlewin.com[1]

---

1. http://www.sarahlewin.com

Chapter One

I shivered as a cool breeze lazily curled around my lower leg, making the exposed skin tingle. The wind whispered a warning. I sat on my haunches beside the vegetable patch I'd been weeding, straining to pay attention to its message. Something cold, wet, and sticky touched my skin, just below my leggings. "That tickles!" I laughed as my brown and white terrier pup Sprinkles licked the part of my skin not covered by clothing. He jumped up, his paws on my knees, nearly knocking me over. I gently removed his paws and straightened, my knees clicking in protest as I stretched into a standing position. He responded by trying to jump as high as he could, as I steadied myself. I leant on the post, along which I'd strung a wire fence at the edge of my vegetable patch.

A rustling in the large mulberry tree in the middle of my backyard distracted me from my pup, as he did his best to convince me it was time for breakfast. The magpies, wagtail birds, and finches darted in and out of the leafy green branches. The orange flash of light as something moved at speed along a branch caught my eye. A couple of weeks ago pumpkins had come to life and disrupted the Halloween festival, but why would a pumpkin be up a tree in my backyard?

The wet lick of my excitable, hungry pup made me smile. "Come on then, let's have breakfast." Sprinkles led me to the kitchen door, where my budgie chirped his normal greeting. "Hi Bert, let me fill up your seed bowl. I'll clean up your cage this afternoon, after my other chores are done." After seeing to Bert, I bent to pat Cinnamon, my light gingery coloured cat, patiently waiting for her morning meal.

Ten minutes later I sat sipped my second coffee, smiling at the bonding in front of me. "You're the best feline ever," I crooned to Cinnamon, who sat patiently waiting for Sprinkles to stop running around in circles and settle. As she began her regular cleaning ritual her protégé copied, licking his paws with his big floppy pink tongue. I wiped away the drop of salty water as it ran down my cheek. Happy tears. Home. In my cottage in amongst the overgrown trees and flowers. Family. The furry and feathered variety. A motley menagerie. My hot tears ran down my cheeks. Tears of happiness. "It took nearly forty years," I whispered to my companions, "But I think I'm finally where I belong."

I tried to keep to my morning routine. It helped me stay on track. I'd been called a control freak on more than one occasion. I hid my anxiety in rules, plans, projects and organisation. "Tomorrow is book club. After I run my errands, we'll finish reading the book." My pets loved the sound of my voice, luckily, my habit of talking aloud helped ease my fears. Cinnamon rubbed against my legs as I sat at the kitchen table writing my list of things to do while I was out.

Moving to Misty Vale, I made a commitment to myself, to not hide away. The book club met fortnightly. In addition to talking about the chosen book, there were often baking, craft tips, free plants, and gossip involved in these meetings. I scribbled some reminders on my spiral bound notebook. To take along some rosemary cuttings, a gingerbread man knitting pattern, and cake or biscuits to share.

As I stood, I caught a glimpse of my reflection. Why the previous owner chose to glue a mirror on the end of the corner kitchen cupboard I'd no idea. My plan to try to remove it, was another item on my list for home improvements. I gently extricated a couple of pieces of stray green leaves from my messy pile of brown hair. The specks of grey didn't bother me. Wound up in a half bun, half ponytail, to keep it out of my face when I worked in the garden, knitted, baked, or pretty much any activity that required concentration. My green eyes stared back at me, tentatively. I cast a critical eye over my top half, making sure there were no more remnants of the tomato or basil plants I'd been pruning.

My skin contained few wrinkles, and my hair still held most of its natural colour, unusual for a forty-year-old. Since I'd moved to Misty Vale I found gardening, knitting, reading, and baking occupied most of my time. *There's nothing wrong with tame pursuits Jane.* After a chaotic career in law enforcement and then as a private eye, a quieter existence might be just what I needed.

I caught sight of another flash of orange, this time outside the kitchen window. I stood, peering out through the screen, but saw nothing unusual. Sprinkles, who barked at everything, hadn't made a sound, so it probably wasn't anything to worry about. "I'm going out for a while," I told my menagerie. Cinnamon glanced up from her kitchen cushion and continued to preen herself. Sprinkles stood in front of me, tail wagging, hoping to join me, and Bert picked at his bell, which made a jangling sound. I checked my patchwork bag, to ensure it contained my keys, wallet, phone, a recyclable carry-all and my notepad, before locking the door.

I took a deep breath, rubbing my hands along the lavender and rosemary bushes I'd planted, inhaling their fragrance. While I'd fallen in love with the property, the front garden consisted of a few tuffs of deadish grass when I moved in. It made me happy, that the fragrant plants in front of me were there because I'd dug the dirt, watered and fed them. I'd plant a few rose bushes next, then jasmine, and maybe geraniums.

The previous owners had painted the weatherboard a pastel lilac. Other homes on either side of the road were painted in similar pastel hues. I made a mental note to pick up some paint next week and give mine a refresh. My heart skipped a beat, my little home in Misty Vale, made me smile as much now as when I'd first set eyes on it, fallen in love with it, and on impulse decided to buy it, six months ago, on my thirty eighth birthday.

I set my pedometer watch as I closed my front gate. *I can do this.* The mantra I invoked every time I left the property, where I felt safe and protected. Nothing in our little village was going to harm me, but for years, on the run from people who didn't understand why sparks of electricity flew when I was upset, or how me walking through a door could cause a strong wind, meant I needed to calm my anxiety each time I ventured outside. People in Misty Vale seemed more accepting, so far. This village was different. People here didn't exactly hide their magic, but it wasn't in your face either. In other places where I lived, briefly, people without powers tended to want to run those with skills out of town or take advantage of them. Those with powers made spectacles of themselves in the bigger cities. I'd lived on edge for years.

The skin on the back of my skin felt clammy, the sun threatened to burn through the light material of my shirt. *Welcome to summer in Australia.* I reminded myself. Time to get used to Christmas in the heat. No snowmen and cozy dinners in front of the fire. The idea of turning back and burying myself in the book was tempting.

No excuses, I can do this.

I preferred to avoid talking to people. If I wasn't interrogating them, I just didn't know how to behave. I'd been like this forever. I suffered panic attacks, and I used to think there was something horribly wrong with me. Other people seemed to be able to hold down a conversation, to go out and share a meal with friends or family and not start tapping their feet after ten minutes. I'd spent so long running from people that it took all my will power to join a crowd, rather than disappear into one. I knew I overreacted in the past, that not everyone judged me for the elemental magic I possessed. *The magic that I didn't understand and didn't know about, because no one told me.*

Counting my steps from my little cottage to the main street, aptly named Spirit Road, helped calmed my anxieties. *I'm not a freak. Other people also possess the power to manipulate the elements.* My positive self-talk was easier to believe now that I lived in a place where other people weren't persecuted for similar abilities.

Determined to keep moving forward, I literally counted my steps along the way to the main street. I'd promised myself, when I moved into Misty Vale, to not become a recluse. I found it easier than I'd imagined to walk ten thousand steps a day, beating my hereditary high cholesterol, pre-diabetes and being fitter than most of my last forty years.

"Looking good Jane." I waved as old Mr Quin called to me from the middle of his rose garden. Seated on his green plastic garden seat, thick orange gloves protecting his hands from the thorns as he inspected his plants for bugs. Nearly thirty years my elder, and as spritely as someone half his age, I admired his dedication to independence.

"Hi Mr Quin, do you want anything from the shops?" I knew he grew most of his own fruit and vegetables in his back garden, harvesting and preserving as much as he could.

"I'm fine, but thanks for asking. After I get rid of these pesky mealy bugs, I'm off to play chess at the hall, with the oldies." He pinched a couple of leaves, squishing the bugs between his gloved fingers.

I smiled as he called his friends 'oldies.' "Have fun."

I walked next few blocks without saying a word, though I waved and smiled at everyone I passed. They waved and smiled back. Living in a village was worlds away from living in the bigger cities. No one was anonymous here.

Chapter Two

"Jane Fairweather! Are you hiding in the wool section?" I cringed as Florence Hartly yelled from the front of the store. With her short stylish bob of dyed blonde, wearing a flashy red summer dress, the self-appointed town matriarch loved being in charge. I'd hoped she'd forgotten she'd spied me as I hurried past her, looking for some wool to make gingerbread men for Christmas. There were far too many shades of brown to choose from. It should have been an easy task. I'd finally chosen a brown that wasn't too dark or too light, with just the right hint of ginger.

I considered my options. If I innocently walked in the opposite direction, pretending I didn't hear her, she'd probably wait at the front of the store for me to leave, or worse, come and find me. A shiny red yarn caught my eye. The colour would be perfect for my Santa and Mrs Claus project. Next to the red, the Christmas tree green wool sat there, looking at me. I tucked one ball of green in my arms, next to where the brown and red sat, wishing I'd thought ahead and grabbed one of their shopping baskets on the way in. Flustered, I'd forgotten my patchwork bag contained an empty reusable shopping bag.

A sigh escaped my lips. I balanced the wool in my left arm, and turned towards the end of the aisle, in the direction of Florence's voice. "Yoohoo Jane, don't forget our book club meets tomorrow at my place. Please be a dear and bring a plate of your famous lemon slice." Great idea, my slice was easier than the cake I was thinking of baking.

"There you are." As soon as I rounded the end of the aisle, Florence waved. It wasn't possible not to see her, I waved back and walked the few metres to meet her in front of the candy canes in their prominent position on the front of the first aisle, the closest to the cash registers. "I'm so glad I found you; it saves me a phone call later. 10am tomorrow, my place. If you can bring some of your lemon slice that'd be perfect. Now I really must dash, I've got to meet Penelope and choose some flowers for the church." The woman in charge of everything in the town turned and bustled to the counter, in a flurry and a flutter, lace, ribbon, and tinsel flying. As if she floated on her own cloud, the whoosh of the air in her wake nearly knocked the balls of wool from my arms.

I shifted the weight of my goodies in my arms and lined up behind her at the counter. At least ten years older than me, maybe more, she carried herself well. Morning Pilates, another activity she tried to recruit me for, kept her in good shape. Her tongue and wit, both as sharp, meant many people bent to her will.

Just like supermarkets with lollies placed invitingly at the checkout, our local craft store, *The Crafty Owl* cleverly showed off cute little do it yourself kits, and other essential craft items. I grabbed a packet of googly eyes, fluffy red, white, and green pompoms, some foam balls, and coloured cardstock. My fingers cramped, holding the packets firmly, waiting for Florence to finish chatting with Cathy.

"Good morning Jane," Cathy Cowan, the owner of *The Crafty Owl* smiled at me. A few years younger than me, she'd visited the town on holiday and decided to move to Misty Vale. Many residents loved their crafts, buying wool, materials, cotton etc online, or venturing into the city. When Cathy set up the craft shop, residents opted to buy locally. Cathy expanded her stock to include all the trinkets and difficult to find bits and bobs normally only available over the internet.

"Good morning Cathy. I love the vibrant wool you've brought in," I unloaded my goodies onto the counter.

"I thought you'd like them," Cathy's eyes lit up. "I can't wait to make something Christmassy myself. I'm not as talented as you. I'd love to see what you make next."

"Nonsense, you've won more ribbons at the local show than I did," I countered. "Are you running any workshops between now and Christmas?" Small talk was not my favourite past time, but I did love learning new crafty skills.

Cathy handed me a trifold flyer. "Here are the times and dates of the workshops between now and the end of the year. I've added more shelves along the walls since the last workshop, with a much wider variety of embellishments, materials, paints and glitter. By Christmas we'll have a 3D printer on a bench next to the cutting machine bench. Members of the crafty club will be able to use either machine, free of charge," Cathy's propensity for building anything, creating amazing products from random items was truly magical. The room where she held craft workshops fitted eight people comfortably. A waiting list of people for her workshops, a testament to how popular they were.

I stepped out of the shop, blinking as the sunlight shone directly at me. I turned left, longing to head home as quickly as possible, to avoid any other conversations. To my right, two doors down from Cathy's shop sat *The Milky Bar.* Misty Vale's most popular café. The trays of cookies and cakes, cupcakes and more, assured a steady stream of customers, of all ages. I honoured my promise, not to run and hide.

My mouth watered as I opened the door, and a wave of sweet sugary aromas hit my nostrils. Jessica Smith had taken ownership of the café from her mother, who still baked daily, and helped during the busier times. They were always trying new recipes. My current favourite were the orange cupcakes. The café was a buzz with customers. I hesitated, halfway into the café, not keen to get caught up in conversation.

Jane Fairweather you'll never get over this curse if you don't make an effort to be around people. Being an empath is part of your magic, embrace it, don't shy away from it. Talking to myself, became a habit, that kept me safe, grounded, and reasonably sane. Discovering that numerous Misty Vale residents were skilled in magic, added to my reasons to stay. My magic didn't always work properly, but at least I'd stopped running. Watching others use their gifts without fear, made me wonder if maybe I wasn't cursed after all.

I'd never asked about my abilities. My parents hadn't shared one piece of information about the skills that must've been passed down from them. Years of research, and paying attention, helped me realise I wasn't as much of a freak as I'd been labelled. Still, fear and hurt are strong motivators for hiding myself away.

The customers in *The Milky Bar* were quieter than I expected, crowded around a long table in the middle of the room. I moved closer, to see what kept everyone away from their cakes and cuppa. I grabbed a quick breath in as I watched a little gingerbread man and a gingerbread woman building a gingerbread house. I could see no strings or wires, or puppeteer under the table controlling it all.

Magic. As far as I understood it, those who possessed special abilities didn't normally use them so publicly. No rule forbade inhabitants from practicing their skills, but generally these displays of magic were kept to smaller closeknit groups, not out in the open for all to see.

My brain whirred away trying to provide a logical explanation for what my eyes were seeing, as the chimney was placed atop the sloped roof, the gingerbread man and woman, icing smiles wide on their faces, gave a little bow and curtsy respectively. I moved away from the display, letting my eyes run over the glass cabinet displaying the biggest range of cupcakes in town.

"Good morning Jane," Jessica smiled as she stood behind the glass cabinet. "I know you love our orange cupcakes; would you like to try one of our new jaffa cupcakes? They're a delicious blend of chocolate and orange," she pointed to a brand-new glass cabinet on the left of the other one. Alongside the jaffa cupcakes were coffee cremes, peppermint patties, and strawberry pies.

"Hi Jessica. The new flavours sound delicious. Can I have one of each to take home, and I'll have a jaffa cake now, with a mocha please." My mouth watered at the thought of the sugar laden goodies. I didn't know whether to comment on the gingerbread house building demonstration.

"Mummy, can we buy the gingerbread people? Can they build us a gingerbread house?" A little girl with blonde curly ringlets tied high up in pigtails, tugged on her mother's dress. Both wore matching pink dresses with skirts of layered tulle and sequins, reminding me of old-fashioned Christmas dolls.

Jessica walked around the counter and crouched down in front of the little girl. "I'm sorry sweetie, but they're not for sale. Next week, I'll have some gingerbread in the café. And some cute little gingerbread houses you can make yourself at home," she stood, lifting a wicker basket off the countertop. "How about you choose one of my special magic cookies, close your eyes, put your hand in and pick one." I watched as the girl gently placed her hand into the basket. I drew in a breath as she pulled out a gingerbread girl cookie dressed in the same outfit as the little girl, complete with sparkly pink bows in its hair.

"You do have gingerbread," the little girl's eyes sparkled with excitement.

"Just for you," Jessica beamed, putting the basket back on the top of the counter. She turned to me. "If you'd like to find a seat, I'll bring your order to you." I smiled my thanks and found a corner booth from where I could watch people coming and going.

As my fellow customers returned to finish their morning tea, I heard muted giggling, as I caught an orange flash out of the corner of my eye. Were there elves running around town? Not unheard of, but I thought elves and fairies normally kept to themselves. I shrugged, not my problem, no longer in law enforcement. "This jaffa cake and mocha are delicious," I said as Jessica walked past carrying empty plates.

The café owner grinned, "Thanks so much Jane."

"The gingerbread people, were they your idea?" I asked, deciding there was no harm in asking.

Jessica sat the plates on the empty table next to mine. "I wish I could take credit for it, but no, they just appeared this morning. The customers loved it. I figure they came from the same place as the Halloween pumpkins and ghosts."

"They were great," I agreed as I headed towards the door. "Very entertaining." So why did my spidey senses tell me that something odder than usual was going on in town?

Chapter Three

I sat the box of treats in my bag, on top of my purchase at the craft shop. Remembering my interaction with Florence I wished I'd thought to buy enough cupcakes for the book club the following day. Not that I minded making lemon slice. It meant I got to keep these yummy treats for myself.

Two thousand steps to my cottage, a few blocks over from the main street. My terrier pup Sprinkles waited at the gate, his tail wagging. "Hey little guy, I'm so lucky I found you, or did you find me?" A few weeks after moving into the cottage, a deceased estate, that came with the cat and the budgie, I'd found the pup on my doorstep. No one claimed him, so I decided he may as well stay. On the day I found him, he'd followed Cinnamon up onto the kitchen bench where I was baking. Less agile than his feline friend and full of puppy bounciness he managed to knock an open packet of hundreds and thousands, tipping most of the contents on himself and the benchtop. In a stroke of good fortune, I'd relocated the iced cupcakes onto the sideboard moments before.

I bent to pat him with my free hand. "Let me get this lot inside and I'll throw your ball with you." His tail wagging, my faithful pup followed me as I unlocked the door and placed the bag gently on the kitchen table.

Cinnamon wrapped herself around my legs, purring. "Finding you in my herb garden was such a blessing! I'll put my goodies away and we'll play ball." Eight furry feet traced my footsteps, as I placed the cakes in the cake tin on the bench and dropped the wool into my woollen bin in the corner behind my armchair.

Bert whistled at me as I picked out a ball from the collection of pet toys near the backdoor. "You'd like to play ball too," I crooned to my grey blue budgie. From the safety of his cage, on a hook near the back door, too far from the bench for Cinnamon to jump to, Bert watched the antics. The tingling sensation in my fingers and toes distracted me, as the magic I'd been cursed with buzzed around my body. *Blessed not cursed.* I reminded myself. Nearly twenty years after my then fiancé had yelled that my magic was a curse that ruined our life together, the wound still burned. I'd run, not understanding that I wasn't the only one who possessed powers.

Cinnamon knocked the ball at my shin. I kicked it back to her, refocusing on my present surroundings. My country cottage kitchen with its wooden pine bench and matching table. The chairs with blue and white cushions that matched the curtains. The wooden hutch with floral plates and bowls neatly stacked on its shelf. I was safe. I counted my blessings daily. The miniature grandfather clock that sat on my mantle chimed eleven. An item I'd collected on my travels, reminding me that there were good memories as well as bad.

Those were dark times, running away, drinking too much, and hiding. Finding work, as a policewoman, helping others and investigating mysteries, ultimately led me here. I laughed as Sprinkles ran in circles around my feet. Cinnamon, curled up on my favourite chair, tired of playing, but still involved, a sly slit eye watching her canine brother expel his remaining energy.

If I made the lemon slice now, it'd set in the fridge while I finished the required reading for book club. Then I could knit for the rest of the day, guilt free, knowing I'd completed my tasks for the next day. Sprinkles and Cinnamon, content with the treats I'd given them, sat watching me, up to my elbows in cookie crumbs and coconut when a sudden thumping at the front door startled me. My hands slipped, dropping the wooden spoon into the slice bowl.

"Hold your horses, I'm coming, just let me wash my hands." Whoever was incessantly knocking on my door, either couldn't hear me or didn't care. Wiping my arms with my hand towel, I opened the front door. My neighbour, Margot Winters, nearly fell in on top of me. Not so steady on her feet since her fall a few months ago. "Margot, come in, I'll make us a cup of tea. Did you forget your walking stick? You really shouldn't travel anywhere without it." I wasn't sure whether to take her arm or if she'd pull away. At seventy-seven, she was still terribly independent. Her short grey hair always neat and tidy, she wore makeup and dressed in cute matching shirt and pants sets. Today's outfit a Christmas themed set with snowmen and Santas set against a light green fabric.

"Pish, posh, I haven't got time for tea. I've just seen the strangest thing, in my garden, and I need you to call the police," Margot's voice rose excitedly.

Worried she'd trip over Sprinkles, as he enthusiastically ran in circles around our visitor, I tried to direct her through to the kitchen. "Please, at least come and sit down at the kitchen table while we wait for the police. You can tell me what's wrong while I finish making a slice for book club tomorrow."

Reluctantly, Margot let me manoeuvre her to a seat in the kitchen. "I haven't got time for this. I need you to ring the station and ask Ned to come out and take away the snowman, his singing is rather awful."

Before I could ask if she meant Ned, our local policeman was singing, or the snowman, I heard a commotion in the garden. I opened the back door in time to see a snowman roll through the gate between my garden and Margot's. He tipped his hat at me, as he strolled past, singing a Christmas carol about his ancestor. I watched, his red scarf trailing behind him, his carrot nose pointing ahead, his arms, branches from a tree, waving as he rolled down beside the house. I ran to my front door in time to see him roll out my front gate and turn right, in the direction of town. I closed both doors, switched the kettle on and turned to my neighbour, Sprinkles at her feet, wagging his tail for attention. "I don't think we have to worry about calling the police."

"Bobs and bells, where did he come from and where's he going? That's what I want to know. I didn't create him."

I touched Margot reassuringly on her arm. "I'm sure no one will think you did." My neighbour's ability to create practical items from rubbish hadn't diminished with age. She sold her creations for a good price, enabling her to stay independent. She didn't scare easily. "Can you tell me what happened?" I poured hot water over a chamomile teabag, Margot's favourite, I preferred lemon and ginger. Placing the mug of steaming tea in front of her, I quickly iced the slice and popped it in the fridge to set. I loved the no bake slices, so simple, quick, and easy.

My neighbour leant forward, then leaned back on her chair, her eyes darting back and forth, recounting the mornings activities in her head. Finally, she spoke aloud. "I went outside to put the drill and the screwdriver back into the shed when I'd finished with them. As I turned to go back inside, the giant snowman started serenading me. I screamed and legged it over here."

"Is that sort of thing unusual, in Misty Vale, at this time of year?" I missed winter Christmases in the UK but was nearly certain I'd not conjured up the singing snowman. "There were enchanted gingerbread people, building a gingerbread house at the café earlier. Pumpkins on the loose during Halloween, I'm curious as to whether Misty Vale is always a little crazy."

Margot stood up. "A little crazy? Ha! Don't you remember the ruckus with the pumpkins, and the trouble the ghosts and the broomsticks caused? Animated like something straight out of a movie, or one of those books the book club reads. But no, we don't normally see random Christmas characters wandering the streets." She sat back down with a thud, not that she weighed much, but her knees wobbled as she landed on the seat. I knew better than to ask if she wanted help. My neighbour was nearly as stubborn as me.

I tried changing the subject. "If you'd like to come along to book club tomorrow, we finished that book, the one you didn't like. We are back to straight forward murder mysteries now, nothing woowoo at all in this one. I can lend you my copy if you like." Margot stopped attending book club when Florence chose one of those cozy paranormal fantasies that were so popular. Our current choice was a hard-hitting murder mystery with a twist. I wanted to read the ending before tomorrow, but as I had a copy on my e-book reader, I didn't mind passing the physical copy to my neighbour.

Eyeing the book I held up, Margot reached out her hand. "I do have some free time this afternoon. It's too hot to be doing much in the garden, I suppose I could give it a go," she said grudgingly. I passed the book to her. The elderly lady turned the book over, studying the cover. "No magic or witchy nonsense in it at all?" She frowned over her glasses at me.

"None at all," I assured her, smiling. She was a sweetie underneath all her bluster. I hope I was as spritely as her at that age. "More tea?" I held up the kettle.

"No thanks dear. I want to make sure snowy didn't damage any of my garden, then I'm going to have some lunch and check out this book. Is the meeting still at ten at Florence's?"

"Yes, it is, would you like me to pick you up?"

"I'll let you know," Margot marched to the back door, and slipped out, going through the gate the snowman had used, shutting it firmly shut behind her.

Chapter Four

My little living room reminded me of the snug in my cottage in Scotland. The armchair I'd found at a garage sale fitted the space perfectly. Comfy to snuggle up in, my knitting chair was a sturdy old style wooden piece of furniture older than me. I'd a blanket for the cooler weather, and the lightweight patchwork fabric meant it didn't scratch or itch during the hotter days. My little cottage had no central heating or cooling. I could use the open fire if needed, although I considered it impractical and messy. In the rare event of a cold winter, I'd use a small electric heater. My cozy living area didn't need much in the way of cooling either. With doors and windows open a lovely breeze cooled the room. I rarely turned on the little air cooler in the corner.

Sprinkles and Cinnamon followed me to the snug and curled up on their cushions in front of my chair. A fluffy pink one for Cinnamon and a fluffy blue for Sprinkles. Bert didn't mind the peace and quiet, though he often talked to himself when we disappeared from the kitchen.

Instead of picking up my tablet, my hand reached for my notepad and pen. The little shelf that I used as a side table held all sorts of bits and pieces that came in handy. I found myself doodling cute tiny gingerbread people, a snowman and assorted pumpkins; instead of finishing the book to see if I'd correctly guessed the ending.

Misty Vale had a reputation in neighbouring towns as a bespoke tourist destination. Residents used their gifts, manipulating the elements to create craft beers, mouthwatering foods, and stunning crafts.

A popular place for grey nomads and families on caravan camping holidays. So why would one of our residents decide to bring inanimate objects to life now?

Or did this type of thing happen often in the village? Margot didn't think so, but in the café, no one seemed worried about the animated gingerbread people. Maybe it was all innocent fun. I had a habit of overthinking.

I must have dozed off because I woke to Sprinkles trying to jump on my lap, Cinnamon curled up on the back of my chair, and my mobile phone buzzing a tinny version of jingle bells. I shooed Sprinkles away, and lifted Cinnamon down, as I answered my phone.

I recognised Ned's voice immediately. I'd met our local policeman during my first week in town, waiting in line at the cafe. It came up in conversation that I'd worked as a private investigator, trained in the UK, under a crochety older retired police superintendent. "I just wanted to let you know, as well as the animated gingerbread people, and the singing snowman, we've had reports of talking reindeer, a couple of elves creating mischief at the school and a scrooge character quoting poetry at the library." He paused, I heard the deep breath he took, releasing it a couple of seconds later.

"I take it this is unusual for Misty Vale. Do you call something like this a breach of the peace or a public mischief?" I couldn't figure out if Ned wanted my help, or whether rounding up characters out of a Christmas pageant sounded like fun.

I heard the frustration in Ned's voice. "Not the norm at all. I'd hoped Halloween was a one off. I'm keen to get to the bottom of what's happening and why. Can you lend a hand Jane? Your specific skillset might come in handy. If you're free of course. I could use a second set of eyes on this."

It took me a second to find my voice, no one had ever asked me to help based on my magical abilities. My fiancé, and others made it clear that my skills weren't normal. "Before I moved here, people considered my unusual attributes a curse, annoying, or irritating."

"Then it's a good thing you're here. Our village accepts we're all different. In this instance I'm referring to your ability to puzzle through a riddle and solve a mystery," Ned replied.

I felt the heat rise in my cheeks, still not comfortable with praise. I preferred to just get on with the job at hand. "Oh that. Okay. I'll put the kettle on, if you're free to fill in some details for me."

Our local policeman was easy to look at. He stood a little over six feet tall, with thick, dark, wavy hair, he reminded me of one of the actors I'd had a crush on for years. His deep brown eyes sent shivers down my spine whenever I looked into them. He lifted his cap and scratched the top of his head. "I don't think there's harm in animated storybook characters, but I'd like to know what's going on, and why. I'd hoped the pumpkins and broomsticks during Halloween were a one off. I wasn't expecting Christmas themed chaos, not that they are causing any mischief, yet." Ned sipped his tea, before taking a bite of lemon slice. I always made a double batch, I had plenty left for bookclub.

"I keep seeing elves, at least I think they're elves. Little flashes of orange just out of my field of vision." I dunked my peppermint teabag in and out of my mug.

Ned scribbled in his notepad. I appreciated that he still used an old-fashioned notepad and pen, rather than an electronic tablet. "You and about seven others, all reported little flashes of orange, and that's just today. Since Halloween reports of strange occurrences have increased about tenfold."

I filled a plastic container with lemon slice for book club, keeping some in a separate tin, in case I received more visitors. "At the café this morning a couple of cute gingerbread people were building a house. Do you think these instances are something we should be concerned about? Margot wasn't happy about the snowman that appeared in her back garden."

"I'm not sure. I was hoping you could help me with that part. I lost the snowman, he's gone quiet, or melted or wandered off into the bush somewhere," Ned flipped through a few pages of his notepad. "I wouldn't call you a gossip, but the other women in the book club are known for being chatterboxes. Can you chat or rather listen to them, see if they have any idea what's happening. I know I said it was your brain and not your magic skills that I needed, but if your intuition kicks in, it'd be appreciated," he grinned sheepishly.

"You're lucky I've a thick skin," I grinned right back. "I'm not offended, I enjoy the sleuthing part, keeping my brain active. Book club is tomorrow, I'll come by the station afterwards if I learn anything useful."

"Righto," Ned stuck his cap back on his head. "Thanks." I would've reached out and touched his arm as I led him to the door, but I didn't think it appropriate. I let my energy vibrate round my body as I smiled, recalling the conversation. There was no harm in looking. I enjoyed his company.

As I cleaned the kitchen and gathered the items together for book club, I found myself daydreaming about the dark, tall handsome policeman. The idea of assisting Ned with a mystery sent my energy buzzing. A few stray streams of light escaped my fingertips. I took a slow breath in, exhaling it slowly. The last thing I needed was a fire in my cottage.

"I enjoy reading, tending to my garden, baking and knitting," I told Cinnamon as I filled her bowl with dried biscuits. "I've enough money to retire on, thanks to my parents' estate, and I'm used to being by myself. Still, I do love a puzzle." Sprinkles sat, his tail wagging furiously, while I poured some doggy biscuits into his bowl, on the other side of the child's gate that separated their bowls.

Determined to finish the book before I did anything else, I read the remaining pages. Only then did I return to my notebook. Starting a fresh page, I listed what I knew, followed by the questions I wanted answered at book club the next day.

Chapter Five

Florence Hartly's house was a ten-minute walk from mine. Margot chose to attend aqua aerobics at the local pool, so I walked the short distance by myself, carrying the plants, slice, books and wools in the calico carry bags I'd sewn at a workshop last year. "The best workshop ever." I told Bert as I tucked everything into the bags before leaving home.

Three snowmen, not as big as the singing snowman of the day before, rolled past me, heading towards the main street. I couldn't help smiling, their little faces full of happiness, with their shiny black button eyes, carrot noses, and crooked stick smiles.

"Did you see the snowmen?" Florence asked as I unpacked my bags onto one of her long grey marble kitchen benches. I was early and the first to arrive. "They bounced past here giggling and singing, creating such a ruckus. It reminded me of the Christmas of 1986, when a whole lot of book characters turned up and hung tinsel and Christmas lights all over the trees in the park."

"What happened back then? Did one of our residents cause the characters to come to life? Does this sort of thing happen often?" Tempted to pull my notebook out of my bag to take notes, I decided that would be a bit much.

"Kids, I think. I can't remember the details. Please place your slice in the middle of the table, thanks." Florence dismissed me, busying herself arranging elegant handmade chocolates on a china plate.

My entire cottage would have fitted into Florence's open plan kitchen and entertaining area. Sharp edges, shiny and silver, dark wood and dark grey trim, it reminded me of a show home. Expensive angular furniture. Bland, without the character of the older buildings in town. The long heavy-set table, set with a golden table runner and matching placemats seated twelve comfortably according to the chairs plotted around it.

"Yoohoo, is anyone home?" Marigold Sparks walked straight in and slipped two trays of sandwiches onto the table. Extricating her floppy straw hat from her curly golden hair, she slung it on the back of one of the chairs. "Constance is picking up Gwennie, they'll be along in a few minutes." She fluffed out her multicoloured skirt as she plopped herself on one of tall formal chairs placed around the table.

I heard the door open before I saw Constance Flowers and Gwennie Gale, both dressed in cream cotton pants and light blue shirts. Older than me by at least ten years, probably more, both had short grey curly hair. I patted the bun I'd managed to create, high up on my head. I'd never mastered the art of perfectly coiffed hair or make up. I sighed; short hair would be even more effort. I didn't even own a hairdryer. Maybe I'd dye my hair purple again, or bright red.

"Sorry we're late," Constance said, catching her breath between words. "All the trees along the road near the shopping centre have giant strands of tinsel and baubles. Everyone slowed driving past to gawk at them."

"Harmless fun," Gwennie patted her best friend on the arm. "Ever since kindergarten, you've been distracted by shiny things. Just look at the dust collectors at your house. How does Kev put up with it?"

"Oh, you kidder," Constance retorted. "You've just as bad, lucky your Brian likes to read as much as you do." Her face reddened, "Um, sorry everyone, the weird goings on have us on edge."

Florence bustled around the table, pulling out chairs for us to sit. I took the hint and placed the mugs on the table. Embossed with our names, I had to admit, the gold print on the deep red mugs did look stunning. Florence had a knack for tasking others organising mugs for book club members, t-shirts for the early morning walkers club, individual birthday cards, and anything else she thought of. Marigold always obliged, too well natured to say no to her friend.

"Let's sit. We've got a lot to get through this morning," Florence's energy manifested as tiny specs of sparkly dust, as she motioned to the pot of coffee and the teapot on their grey metal placemats. "Help yourself to tea or coffee. Thanks everyone for coming along and bringing food. Jane, as long as you're happy to make your slice and bring it along to meetings, we don't need the recipe." I nodded, not needing to interrupt as Florence continued. "Please everyone take home some plant cuttings. I can see we have a quite a selection today. Thanks everyone for your contributions." The garden project had been my idea, keen to see what other plants we all grew in our spare time, but I didn't mind Florence running with the idea. "If we're all free one-day next week, I'd like to get stuck into our Christmas projects. I see some of you have brought in patterns, and thank you, but let's dedicate another morning rather than take away from book club."

"Of course, just let us know when you want us here," Constance sounded breathless, flustered.

"A great idea," Gwennie echoed her friend.

Marigold and I nodded our agreement to our leader's suggestion of a dedicated craft session.

"Before we start on the book, as the relative newcomer to the town, I'm curious, has anything like we are seeing, the pumpkins and snowmen coming to life, the giant Christmas decorations, ever happened before?" I figured that would be an innocent enough question.

Gwennie opened her mouth to speak, but Florence was fractionally quicker. "There are occasionally isolated incidents, if someone accidentally animates their decorations."

Gwennie glanced at our host, lost in her own thoughts, sipping her tea. "There was that incident in the eighties, where storybook characters came to life. This feels a little like that."

Constance nodded. "As a kid I kept freezing glasses of water and accidentally melting all the ice cream in the freezer. As I grew older my powers subsided for a while. Now I can control water in ways I never thought possible. Thankfully I haven't flooded anything in years," she giggled nervously. I remembered a story I'd heard about the local pool overflowing and threatening to flood the park, until one of the swimming instructors managed to get the water under control.

"I think we've all found our powers increasing in strength, especially in the last few years," Marigold fiddled with the ruby ring on her right hand. "I haven't started any fires by mistake for so long, I can't remember the last time. As a kid I was always getting into trouble for sending sparks flying when I was upset." Marigold made jewellery and taught metalwork to interested teenagers at the high school. "I'm so glad I can help the oldies in winter," she turned to me. "Did you know I go with Frankie when he delivers firewood, and I help get their fireplaces sorted." Marigold blushed a little, I felt the heat emanating from her, even though I sat on the other side of the table. I knew Marigold's brother Frankie by reputation only, he spent all his time helping around the town, having retired from working on council a few years earlier.

Gwennie's elemental magic had to do with air, I wasn't sure exactly what that meant and she hardly ever spoke about it. "My gift has changed over the years too," she spoke so quietly I leant forward to hear her. "I'm able to propel people forward, to the best decisions or to take the next step with something," she blushed. "I guess that's why I'm still working at the wellness centre, people come and find me and talk to me."

I knew Florence's skill had to do with managing people. "I just boss people around," Florence grinned unashamedly. "My family are earth elementals. You, my dear Jane are a dark horse. You're a spirit element but with other traits as well."

I nodded, not knowing what to say. "My story, I promise I'll tell it another time. Suffice to say I didn't grow up knowing or understanding my magic. That's partly why I ask so many questions now. Questions like who in town is likely to be bringing decorations to life and why? Has there ever been sinister magic in the town or at least anyone with less than noble ulterior motives?" I picked up a chocolate covered strawberry, popping in my mouth before I said anything else.

Florence and the others exchanged knowing glances around the table, before she spoke. "People use magic for a variety of reasons, sometimes just for fun. Maybe someone is trying to spread some innocent Christmas cheer." Florence popped a chocolate strawberry in her mouth, as she turned to Marigold.

"It's a challenge, to work out whether people should be reprimanded for using their magic for the wrong reasons. I mean, who's going to make that call? I'm on the town council, we don't have a mayor, our council is run collaboratively. We keep an eye on things, but we don't punish people for using their magic, like some other towns do. We let Ned and Sophie enforce the law. It works well," Marigold concurred.

"That makes sense," I wanted to make notes, but I knew that'd be rude. Luckily my memory was still pretty good. I'd fill a page or two with the info as soon as I returned home. I sensed Marigold and Florence were holding back, even Gwennie and Constance were uncharacteristically quiet. "Does the council would keep track of everything? If there was an issue, would they step up, or leave it to the police? I just like knowing how things work."

"We know in general which families have gifts and which element or power they possess. It's not a register as such. As you'd imagine some families possess more powers than others, but that information is not something we share with anyone else," Marigold's tone took on a serious note.

"Thanks for sharing as much as you have. I appreciate it. That's my curiosity answered. Apologies for the twenty questions." I tried for a light hearted tone, but seeing Florence's gaze on me, I wasn't sure it was successful. Wisdom told me not to ask any additional questions.

"If we're finished providing a history of our town, maybe we can get started on the book." Our hostess held up her copy of this week's book.

Chapter Six

An hour later the mystery of the murder and mayhem in a fictious village in the UK had been pulled apart and analysed. We'd chosen the next book, from a short list of three, a small-town baker and mystery solver won out against a romantic comedy set on a cruise ship, and a book about a coven whose spells caused a commotion in the city where they lived.

"Does Misty Vale have covens and people who cast spells?" I wondered aloud. There was still so much to learn. I noticed a subtle glance between the other women.

"Not formal, full on witchy covens like you've seen on television or read in books," Florence said curtly.

Surprised at our hostess's abrupt tone I added hastily. "I didn't mean to offend anyone, I'd never thought about it, even though I've lived here a while. I guess all the talk about magic, and one of our book options being about a coven...sometimes my mouth speaks before I think about what I'm going to ask."

Marigold leant and patted my hand. "We know you didn't mean anything by your questions. You couldn't know the history," she stopped abruptly as someone kicked her under the table. I felt the rush of air as the offender moved quickly.

Florence frowned at Marigold, then sighed. "What she means is, in the past, there have been people who've formed covens and cast spells, a little like we see in the movies," she conceded. "Our grandmothers, mine and Marigold's, it was long ago." Another glance, this time at the friends on the other side of the table. "I'm sure there are people who dabble in this kind of craft even today, though it's rare that anything untoward is the result." My intuition told me she only told me a fraction of what she could.

The temperature in the room dropped. Sun shining in through the window cast warm pockets on the cream tiles. The sudden coolness seemed unrelated to the weather. For the first time since joining the book club I wondered about the members. Before I could unpick my thought any further Florence's mobile beeped. She picked it up, tapped the keyboard and walked towards the door that led to the hallway and the rest of her house. "Excuse me, but I have to take this."

Marigold's phone beeped a few seconds later. Her cheeks turned as red as the lace on her skirt as she read the screen.

"Oh my gosh Marigold, what's wrong? You look like you've seen a ghost." Constance patted Marigold's hand. She withdrew her hand quickly, as the heat from her friend's cheek spread throughout her body.

"Oh, I'm sorry. I didn't mean to hurt you," Marigold's voice quivered, taking a deep breath in and exhaling. "My control is getting better, except when I'm upset," she pointed to her phone. "There's been a fire at the storage lockers in the old warehouse, next to the broom factory. No one was hurt, but there's significant damage," Marigold stood. "Our town welcomes everyone and is forgiving and inclusive, but when there's an incident like this, they always blame the gifted."

I got up from the table and collected our empty mugs and plates. "Do a lot of residents have the same types of skills? Sorry I know that sounds dumb."

Constance collected the plates of food and returned them to their plastic containers. "It's not a dumb question. You didn't grow up here wouldn't know this stuff. The answer is yes, we're all a little different, but many of us share similar skills. When groups gather to combine their skills, it can be dangerous, though people rarely mean to cause trouble..." her voice trailed off as Florence returned to the room, the thunder in her face evident, even from the other side of the room.

Quick as a flash she plastered a smile on her face. "Thanks for tidying up. I need to go meet Penelope. The Country Women's Club have a storage locker in the warehouse. We must make sure it's not damaged. We'll reconvene same time next fortnight, happy reading." As she spoke, she rounded each of us up under the pretext of a hug, ushering us out her front door. I didn't mind leaving the lemon slice behind, I'd pick up the container next time.

"Can I offer you a lift?" Constance asked as she and Gwennie hopped into her pale blue VW bug.

"Thanks, but I'd rather walk, it's not far." I waved as they drove away.

As I walked past Marigold's orange sedan, she leaned over and grabbed my hand. "It was lovely to chat today," she said a little too loudly, as the door to Florence's garage opened, letting out her dark blue Mercedes, before slowly closing. As Florence waved to us both, Marigold placed her hands on the steering wheel, and started her car which flew down the road so quickly it left me breathless. I kept my hand closed around the note she'd tucked into my palm, waving to Florence with my free hand, as I headed home.

After Florence's car turned the corner, I uncrumpled the note. *4pm at 23 North Street.* Did Marigold want to me to tell me something she couldn't say in front of the others? Did she live in North Street, or did a coven meet there at 4pm? My head spun at the strange behaviour of my fellow book lovers once I mentioned covens and spells. Or was it my imagination?

I turned left towards the police station, instead of right which would have taken me home. I didn't have anything specific to tell Ned, but I'd said I'd call in afterwards. I'd tell him what I'd learnt and get to see his handsome face again.

Would he even be at the police station? He'd probably be out investigating the fire. I knew the warehouse and broom factory was on the other side of town, a few streets back from the main street, on the way to the river. The broom factory itself more of a tourist attraction than a small business, though the handmade millet brooms were popular.

If I planned to walk there, I'd need a drink. A cold drink, not an alcoholic one. Egg nog in a little pub in Scotland had been the last time I'd indulged in any kind of alcohol. I smiled, as I passed the local pub, a white brick building where old timers stood on the verandah, glasses in one hand, and hand rolled cigarettes in the other. "Definitely a cold non-alcoholic drink," I muttered, smiling at the friendly, if a little ratty, bunch of men hanging on the rails.

Rather than risking the temptation of grabbing an iced tea at the bakery, where the sugary, sparkly cupcakes would call to me, I opted for a bottle of water from *The Crafty Owl*. I knew Cathy kept some at the counter at the checkout, so I didn't even have to walk past the rows of craft items that would distract me.

"Just the water Jane, or can I get you something else?" Cathy asked with a smile.

"Nothing else today, thanks. I decided to go for a walk, and I forgot my bottle. I thought I'd head towards the river. It's a nice day." It was only a little fib, still I felt guilty.

"Just be careful," I heard the concern in the shop keeper's voice. "Did you hear about the fire at the warehouse?"

"Yes, I heard," I saw an opportunity to learn more information. "I've seen snowmen walking around the streets, is that usual for this time of year? I'm curious, being new, this is my first Christmas here? Does this sort of thing happen often?"

I couldn't pick the look that crossed Cathy's face, before her smile reappeared. My intuition told me she knew something she wasn't going to share with me. "It happens, from time to time. People experiment with their powers. It's generally not a big deal," she brushed off her earlier concern about safety. "I didn't mean to alarm you earlier, I merely meant it's hot outside and it's a long walk to the river, there'll be people driving around to look at the warehouse."

At that moment a young mum with a pram wheeled up to the counter, the top of the pram laden with fabric and wool. I left as Cathy helped her customer with her craft items. More puzzled than ever, I wished I knew more about my powers and the magic that other people possessed. Why did I feel that I was walking into a trap?

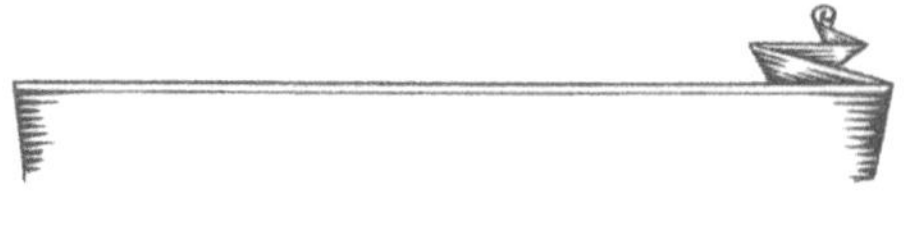

Chapter Seven

Two large reindeer stood blocking my way. In their defence, they probably didn't mean to, they were tethered by their reins to the signpost alerting me to mind my step at the entrance to the *Misty Vale Broom Factory*. With police, fire, and ambulance vehicles at the old warehouse, my idea to investigate via the broom factory seemed valid. Millet brooms were still hand stitched at this historical site, with opening hours 9am until 1pm Monday through Saturday. Roman and his son Leo, owner operators of the small family business approached me from behind the magnificent creatures. Both tall, broad shouldered, Roman's black hair peppered with grey, while Leo's was tied back in a long ponytail. They walked around the side of the handsome animals, so as not to startle them. I took a step backwards, Reindeer were much bigger and intimidating in real life. Not as cute as their storybook counterparts.

Roman played bagpipes in the town band, his son a drummer in a local band; I'd met them both at the nursery when I was looking for unusual varieties of herbs. "It's Jane, isn't it? Thanks for the recommendation, our roses are growing nicely." Roman gestured to the animals standing between us, "I don't suppose you own these beautiful creatures. We tied them up here so their owner could find them. I've no idea where they came from."

"I'm sure someone will claim them; they are interesting looking animals," I peered at the furry brown beasts from as closely as I felt comfortable. "They're not the oddest characters wandering around our little town recently."

Leo grinned. "Yeah, it's crazy. Dad says things like this happen every few years. I was a teenager last time. Were you here about a broom?"

"Now that's a great idea, I do need a new one, but I walked here looking for Ned, and I don't fancy walking a broom home," I smiled. "I'll be back in the morning in my car if that's okay. Can you please put one aside for me."

"Of course," Leo replied. "We're closing now but will be open tomorrow morning."

"Thanks. As I said, I'm looking for Ned, but I can see he's busy at the warehouse. I'll catch up with him later, and I'll keep an ear out for anyone who's looking for reindeer." As I left the broom factory, I debated cutting across the sports field, a more direct route home. It'd been a long day, and I yearned for my cosy chair, a cuppa and a book. I chose instead to head towards the main street and *The Milky Bar*. I couldn't think of a better place to learn about the latest events around town.

"Did you hear the news?" Jessica asked as she delivered a mocha and peppermint choc chip muffin to my booth. The café was full of people eating salad rolls, sandwiches, cakes and pastries.

"The fire at the warehouse? Florance and Marigold told me," I responded, noticing the clock on the wall. It felt later than 1 o'clock in the afternoon.

Jessica sighed. "There's that, but also we seem to have a dozen or more reindeer wandering around town, and there's a problem at the river." The little golden bells jangled above the door, as a group of teenagers walked in, their backpacks slung over their school sports clothes. I dug around in my bag for my notebook. As I sipped my mocha, I made some notes, jotting down everything I could remember from the morning's events. As I read back over what I'd written it became clear that there was a lot I didn't know or understand. Generally, about how our town worked and specifically the recent occurrences. I didn't need to wait long to learn the problem at the river.

"My dad works at the fishing shack, and he said someone turned the water in the river into lemonade. Not the fizzy drink, the original sour drink my grand dad used to make and sell when he was a kid," the teen with the long blonde hair tied into a high ponytail told the others in the group.

"Eww," The shorter girl with the dark hair wrinkled her nose, "Why turn the river into something yuck? I'd choose cola, or red fizzy drink."

"Or chocolate milk," The third teen suggested.

I smiled to myself, thinking it no mean feat to turn the river into lemonade. I was curious how to turn the river back, or who'd have that job. Ned and his team would be busy trying to keep onlookers away.

As I stood, my knees creaked, reminding me I'd walked for longer than normal, having easily made my ten thousand steps. I took my empty plate and mug to the counter. Jessica smiled her thanks, as she whirred ice cream and topping around in her vintage metal milkshake container.

When I moved into my little cottage, the ratty old metal mailbox hung off its fence post, desperately in need of repair. As I occasionally ordered craft items online, before I discovered *The Crafty Owl*, I created a larger mailbox, fashioned to resemble a large knitting basket. I used a black plastic bin, inside an old wicker basket, attaching it to the fence with heavy duty wire. The plastic red flag on the top of the lid stood to attention, signalling mail. "I don't remember ordering anything," I told my eager pup, so pleased to see me he tried his best to knock me over as I opened the gate, juggling the curious package.

Cinnamon greeted me as I unlocked the front door, Sprinkles jumping even higher in an attempt to land in my arms. I dropped the package onto my armchair and led my animals into the kitchen. "Food time for you my patient friends, and a peppermint tea for me. My legs need a rest after all that walking."

A few minutes later, all three of my pets were content with full bellies. The open back door let a cool breeze weave through my cottage as I sat in my chair pondering the parcel. The size of a packet of Christmas fruitcake. I shook it. The sound of a dull thud as its contents shifted from one side to the other didn't provide much of a clue. Neither did the brown paper packaging with no name, stamp or sender details. I unwrapped the string around the package. Like unwrapping the *pass the parcel* game of my childhood. Three layers later I was left with a floral cardboard box, the type you buy from a two-dollar shop. I opened the gaudy orange and pink lid to find another parcel wrapped in brown paper. Using the scissors from my knitting basket I cut gently the sticky tape. The brown paper peeled away, revealing a heavy grey metal key attached to a thick red ribbon. I turned the key over, hoping to reveal a clue, but I found no inscription.

Sprinkles pounced as Cinnamon batted the screwed-up paper in front of my feet. "What've you got there?" I extricated the brown paper before it got too soggy. Sprinkles and Cinnamon, thinking it a game both tried for my lap. "Steady on guys, just let me see if there's anything inside, then you can have it back," I peeled the layers apart carefully, catching a glimpse of white tucked in the side of the second layer. A piece of paper the size of a business card fluttered onto my lap. Satisfied there were no other clues, I scrunched up the paper and threw it for Sprinkles to chase. The words *Misty Vale is a town with secrets. Old, hidden from view, bubbling just beneath the surface is a truth that is fighting to be revealed. You are the key to solving the mystery. The Coven holds the clues you need.*

I turned the piece of paper over, hoping to find a clue on the other side, but found no other words, so I flipped it back to the writing. What secrets and truths were the writer referring to? Why send it to me? Who sent it? How was I the key to solve the mystery? What coven? I rubbed my forehead, squeezing my eyes tight, to clear my brain of the questions swirling around. It didn't help. "There's has to be a practical way, to solve this mystery," I told Cinnamon and Sprinkles, who both looked up expectantly at the sound of their names. As I didn't move towards the kitchen to provide more food, they returned to licking their paws. I opened my notebook, ready to write down everything I knew relating to the weird occurrences over the last few days. I dropped my pen, as the beeping of my mobile startled me.

"Jane, It's Ned, apologies for missing you this afternoon, it turned into quite a busy day."

I grabbed my pen and notebook and headed to the kitchen table. "Don't worry about that Ned, I could see you had your hands full, and that you'd contact me when you had the chance."

I heard the sigh in his voice, an indication of another long day. "Do you know about the warehouse fire, and the issue with the river?"

"The stray reindeer too." I clicked the switch on the kettle after ensuring it contained enough water. "Just boiling the jug if you want a cuppa. There's some lemon slice left too." I returned to my comfy chair, remembering the key. "I need to show you something, if you have a few minutes."

"I can be there in five minutes; I'm on my way to check the progress with the river anyway." He sounded perkier, maybe the offer of some slice, or the clue I now held in my hand.

A few minutes later, we were sitting at my kitchen table; the dashing, tall policeman and me. If I'd been blessed with a relationship, it'd be with someone just like Ned. There was an honesty, a calmness and an inquisitiveness in his aura. Sprinkles sat at his feet, tail wagging as the policeman said hello and found a treat in his pocket to share. Cinnamon, after a general walk by, had returned to her cushion, unperturbed by our visitor.

"Thanks for this Jane, it's just what I needed," he chose a piece of slice from the container I'd place on the table. We sat in comfortable silence, savouring lemon slice and peppermint tea.

"Do you have any idea who's causing the mischief around town? Is it the same person or group of people? Animated Halloween and Christmas characters, reindeer on the loose, the lemonade river, and the arson at the warehouse...it doesn't feel like the work of one person," I mused, referring to my notebook.

"That's the weird thing," Ned reached for a second piece of slice. "The incidents themselves, when you list them like that, sound like different culprits, but at each location, the feeling is the same."

"Can you articulate the feeling? What sense do you get?" I eyed the slice, gave in and added a second piece to my plate.

"Misdirection," Ned picked up a second piece of slice.

"Like a magician?" I asked.

Ned nodded. "We focus on cute characters, and we miss something else that is maybe more important. We spend our resources on an arson attack, and we overlook another crime. A river of lemonade causes a lot of people to look in one direction, while something else is neglected. The incidents are getting a lot of attention, but I get the distinct impression we're all missing something," he grinned lopsidedly, "Or I'm totally crazy."

I pushed the key and the mysteriously worded scrap of paper towards Ned. "You're not crazy," I spoke gently, "This was waiting for me when I got home this afternoon."

Ned turned the key over in his hand, inspecting the metal for any hidden details. He did the same with the red ribbon. After reading the cryptic clue, and examining the paper closely, he returned both items to the table. "Any ideas what this is referring to, or who sent it?"

"Not yet. It appears to have been hand delivered, with no address or clue on the parcel as to who the sender could be. Until this morning I'd not considered the idea that covens existed in the real world, even in a town with magical folk, which was an oversight on my part. When I asked questions this morning at book club, I got the distinct impression they weren't telling me the truth. This note makes no sense. I'm new to town, I've no knowledge of where my magic came from." I thought about the way Florence and the others behaved earlier. "I'm happy to push the ladies for more answers, though I'm not sure how successful I'll be."

Ned's phone rang. A low rumbling buzzing sound that made Sprinkles jump. Cinnamon glanced over but didn't move from her comfy spot. "Excuse me for a minute," Ned strode over to the backdoor, moving into the garden as he listened to what the caller had to say.

I busied myself cleaning the table, suspecting that call would be dragging the policeman away to another incident. I held the weighty key in my palm. What did it unlock? It was too big for a regular door lock. "Honestly, it looks more like it would open an old chest, or a heavy-set wardrobe," I showed Sprinkles as he jumped to see the object.

"I have to go," Ned confirmed, "A few of our local families have been away on a group business trip, and upon returning home, have discovered their homes and businesses have been broken into." He rubbed his hand slowly across his forehead. "Old families, with power and influence. None of them want to come to the station, we have to go to them. There's only the two of us available so Sophie and I will be having a late night."

Choosing a plastic container from my cupboard, I quickly filled it with slice, a couple of apples, and a handful of grapes. "I don't have bread to make sandwiches, but here's a snack for you and Sophie. Is there anything else I can do?"

"Thanks so much! I appreciate it and so will Sophie. In terms of helping, if you could solve the mystery of the key and the paper clue it would be appreciated," he grinned a boyish grin that again made me think how it would feel to touch his cheek, or even to kiss it. I hoped he was too preoccupied to notice the colour I felt burning in my cheeks. "I don't know what's been stolen but all five family representatives were livid over the phone. I'm hoping they'll have calmed down by our visits."

"I'll let you know if I figure anything out," As I opened the front door for Ned, Cinnamon and Sprinkles both rubbed past my shins on the way through. I followed them into the front garden. I clasped my hands together tightly in front of me, resisting the urge to touch the policeman's arm.

"Thanks again for this, and everything," Ned held the container tightly as he manoeuvred past my excitable pup, closing the gate firmly before Sprinkles could join him.

"Good luck." I waved as he climbed into his car and drove away. I half expected to see reindeer wandering down the street.

Chapter Eight

"Oh, my goodness, I nearly forgot," as the grandfather clock chimed three times, the hairs on my arms tingled as I rummaged around in my bag. "Where did I put that note Marigold handed to me?" Sprinkles wagged his tail as he nosed the bag, trying to help. Squeezing my fingers into the pocket of my jeans I retrieved and re-read the crumpled note. *4pm at 23 North Street.*

I tidied the kitchen, and splashed my face with cold water, still flushed after the visit by the handsome policeman. I caught sight of the smile on my face, as my energy buzzed around my body. It's been so long since I'd spent time with anyone of the opposite sex, and even longer since a visit made me smile. I stood a little taller, my face in less of a frown than normal. "I'll be back soon," I told my furry family. Cinnamon didn't stop preening herself, though she did look in my general direction. Sprinkles wagged his tail, hoping I'd take him with me. "Not this time, little fella. I don't know how long I'll be."

North Street wasn't far from my place. I headed left, planning to take a short cut through the park. After only a few steps, a car pulled alongside me. I recognised Marigold's orange sedan before she spoke. "Hop in," she said, leaning over and pushing open the passenger door.

The interior of Marigold's car was surprisingly neat. I don't know what I expected, but as a member of half a dozen local groups that I knew of, I thought there'd be books, boxes, or bags, some evidence of her activity. I clicked my seat belt, my hands tightly clutching my bag on my lap, unsure of how to start the conversation. It wasn't every day that I attended a clandestine meeting about a coven.

"I saw Ned leaving your place, I hope everything is okay," Marigold sounded breathless, less like herself, and I sensed fear, rather than concern.

My sixth sense told me a little white lie would be appropriate. I crossed my fingers, hidden under my bag. "I promised him next time I made lemon slice I'd save him some. He picked some up on his way to work." If she'd been watching, she'd have noticed Ned carrying the plastic container.

My captor, for it felt like I'd been scooped up off the street, muttered something I couldn't quite hear. The dark clouds covering most of the sky, accompanied by a deep rolling thunder added to the threatening atmosphere.

I'm safe, I haven't been kidnapped, this is real life not a murder mystery. The air in my lungs helped calm me, as I took a deep breath in, exhaling slowly. My palms sweaty under my calico bag, as I felt through the fabric. I doubted my phone, wallet, or notebook would make effective weapons.

"I thought we were going to North Street?" I concentrated on keeping the alarm out of my voice as we appeared to be heading towards the burnt warehouse, which was in entirely the opposite direction.

"Florence wanted us to check on something first," Marigold's statement seemed innocent enough. I tried to remember which group she'd spoken about in the context of the warehouse. The two women were involved in quite a few organisations.

Before I could think of a response, we arrived at the scene of the fire. Police tape cordoned off the area, but with no police presence. I knew they'd be busy with the recent spate of break ins. The damage to the warehouse didn't seem too bad up close. The tin walls and roof, erected around a wooden frame, stood tall and proud. The storage facility, separated from the rest of the space by a wooden wall frame and a door, would need more substantial repair. The fire had scorched the wooden structure, warping it. Through what was left of the door, five mesh cages, little more than chicken wire stretched around some metal posts, contained cardboard boxes, striped bags, trestle tables, and plastic chairs. The type of goods for setting up market stalls or sports days. The damage here, appeared to be more from the water damage, rather than the fire itself. "I can't remember which group Florence said had their items stored here, did they lose everything?" I hoped my question sounded harmless.

Marigold frowned at me; her thoughts somewhere else as she rummaged around the soggy cardboard boxes in the first cage. As she didn't answer, I took a few steps to one side, to get a better view of the area. A pile of sodden, burnt items, possibly rags, in the corner, where the wall of the storage area wasn't attached to the warehouse itself, felt...odd. A magic residue emanated from it. Tiny hairs on the back of my neck tingled. Could I make an excuse and leave? A glance at my book club mate advised me caution, and not to make any fast moves. In the second storage cage, Marigold muttered something as she opened a couple of blue, red, and white striped bags. I turned to one side, hoping to pull out my phone and text Ned. The problem is, if she looked up, she'd see what I was doing and I wasn't comfortable with my back to her. I moved towards the door, testing to see if my movement would be noticed.

Marigold frowned at me, no recognition in her eyes. As if in a trance, she tipped out the contents of the second bag. Her hand reached out and picked up something, a book maybe, I couldn't see properly. She tucked it into the leather bag slung around her shoulder. A clunking sound, of something metal hitting the concrete floor, had her diving to retrieve that item as well. Without taking my eyes off Marigold I stepped backwards through the makeshift door that separated the storage area from the warehouse proper.

My heart jumped as a click and a whoosh sound came from the pile of papers on a desk beside me. My nostrils curled at the acrid smell of burning rags near a metal drum. Bright red embers caught my eye to my left, as a flash of red flew past me. Instinct told me that flash was Marigold. It also told me to run. I did. As fast as I could. As the little orange car flew down the street, the blood pounded through my legs as I pushed them, one then the other in big strides until I found my way lit by streetlights. I stopped, panting as I caught my breath, my fingers trembling as I pressed buttons on my phone.

"Emergency. Fire at the warehouse on River Street," I told the operator, not bothering to mask my trembling voice. My body shook as the shock of what had happened caught up with my body, now I'd stopped fleeing for my life. I swung around cautiously, expecting to see the warehouse lit against the late afternoon sky.

I blinked, not believing what my eyes told me, as the warehouse collapsed. I stood a couple streets away, watching, as a wave of water whooshed over the rubble, before returning to where it came. The river I guessed, which sat at the end of the street, a few hundred metres from the warehouse. I turned back towards my home, the second long walk of the day, puzzling out the events I'd witnessed.

The warehouse imploded before the wave; I was certain of that. I flinched at a sudden flash in my peripheral vision caused my heart to pound heavily, again. Christmas lights on the house to my left came to life, complete with tinny Christmas music. The carollers, standing in the garden in the winter woollies, were about a metre tall. A scene from a Christmas card brought to life. Three snowmen, about the same size, zoomed in circles around the garden, throwing snowballs at each other. I shook my head, trying to clear the illusion. Nope, still there. I nodded at the characters, my mouth turned into a smile before I could stop it. Despite everything I'd just experienced, the Christmas scene it front of me, was adorable, in a weird sort of way.

On impulse I turned right at the street before mine. It was nearly dark, but I was curious as to what would be waiting for me at 23 North Street. I had my phone and could call Ned if I needed to, though I suspected he'd still be busy.

From what I could see, the address belonged to an unassuming weatherboard house with a tin roof, mostly hidden behind a huge hedge of prickly purple bougainvillea, imbued with a protection spell. After cutting my hand three times on the thorns, I crossed back to the other side of the road. What I could glimpse of the house, I assumed was a glimmer, a spell to conceal the truth of the property. Letting the witchy vibes propel me away from the location, I headed home.

After patting my furry friends and saying hi to my feathered one, I sat at my kitchen table, a large mug of coffee and the peppermint cupcake I'd been saving for dessert, in front of me. I savoured both, as I allowed my heartbeat to slow to a more normal speed. I knew all too well what happened if I let my fight or flight response get the better of me. Squaring my shoulders, pushing them down, forcing the relaxation, as I exhaled. My energy still ran high, the tingling on my arms told me that. I wiggled my fingers, encouraging the energy to leave in a way that didn't cause an electrical fault anywhere nearby.

You are safe Jane, no one is trying to hurt you, or blame you for anything. You don't have to run. Home is safe.

Slowly, my heart rate returned to a normal pace, it's rhythmic thumping lessened to a quieter level. My breath slowed, in tune with the blood pumping around my body.

My notebook open to a blank page, I scribbled in silence for as long as it took to get the events of the last twenty-four hours down on paper. Another sip of coffee and bite of peppermint. Another breath out. I picked up my mobile and sent a text to Ned. *Not urgent, but we need to talk, tomorrow morning, as a priority.*

I knew that was confusing, but my brain couldn't compute properly. As much as my body tingled, full of nervous energy, I needed sleep, to recharge and calm things. Misty Vale didn't need me to lose my cool.

Chapter Nine

I sat in bed, my eyes refusing to focus on the words on the book in front of me. I'd been delusional to think sleep would come at six in the evening, despite the events of the day. As I climbed out of bed, both Cinnamon and Sprinkles looked at me knowingly and headed back to the snug.

In one corner stood a skinny tallboy. It housed my collection of craft, everything from googly eyes and darning needles to glue and glitter. The crafty spirit of Misty Vale was contagious. The village beckoned me, not only to sit and settle a while, but to use crafts to tap into my creativity. I spent so much time running away, and channelling all my energy into hiding, and investigating crimes, I thought I'd be bored if I settled down. That wasn't the case. Learning new skills, cooking and crafts, fascinated me. There were a never-ending amount of skills to learn and practise.

I held my breath, concentrating on calming my rapid pulse. Did the events of the afternoon mean this was no longer my haven? I hoped not. The last time I'd felt this safe, well, before I stepped into Marigold's car, had been as a child.

At the time, my childhood seemed as normal as everyone else's. An only child, I spent my time reading or playing with imaginary friends. My parents worked full time and were often away. From necessity I taught myself to cook, clean, and look after myself. When my mother wasn't working as an accountant, she helped out at the art studio, teaching still life painting. My father worked at the local supermarket, managing the fresh food section, and taught woodcraft at the local men's shed. When they were home, we spent hours playing card games and board games, My favourite games were the ones with mysteries and puzzles to solve.

Opening the bottom drawer of the tallboy, I extricated the only item left from the first twenty years of my life. I caressed the top of the sturdy, old cardboard box. This travelled with me as I escaped the taunts of people who didn't understand my powers. The key dropped in my mailbox triggered a memory from long ago.

I lifted the lid of the box. "Do you see this picture?" I showed Cinnamon an old photo of the house I grew up in. "In that old shed, there on the left, sat a wooden wardrobe. I think this key would fit that." Cinnamon lost interest, as Sprinkles jumped on his hind legs to see what I was up to. "We're not going on a road trip; the house and shed were renovated a few owners ago," I told him. "Ten hours in a car, to knock on the door and ask some strangers if I can look for an old wardrobe, no thanks," I let a smile play on my lips, as I remembered playing hide and seek amongst the many rooms in my parents' house and in the garden that circled around it. My childhood wasn't so bad.

Inside the box I'd kept a few trinkets. An art deco brooch of my mothers, a little brown leather purse my dad gave me once, and some photos of me as a kid, with my parents. Underneath an old head scarf that depicted the Sydney harbour bridge and the opera house, was a small book. Its thin pages told the story of a small bear and the antics he got up to, traveling the world with a small red suitcase. Hot salty tears ran down my cheeks, landing on my lips. That book, and the tiny toy teddy bear held such fond memories of sitting, hiding in a corner of the garden full of geraniums, azaleas, petunias, and pansies. The family tabby, Gilbert, by my side always.

"I don't remember this." Five small stones sat encased in the dull metal of an antique grey metal ring. A small red stone sat alongside a small green one, followed by a blue stone, an amber coloured stone, with a purple stone completing the circle. The piece of jewellery slid smoothly over the ring finger on my right hand, fitting as if it were made for me. When I tried to slide it off, it stubbornly refused to budge. "I guess I'll just pull it off next time I wash my hands," I shrugged, as Sprinkles licked my hand, trying to help. "I mightn't be able to get to that old wardrobe, but somewhere in this village there must be a clue." As I said it aloud, I realised my pets had wandered off. The question I'd still to answer, one among many, was where in Misty Vale would I find the piece of furniture that fitted the key.

I dialled Ned's mobile number, unsurprised when the call went through to his voicemail. "If you get this message while you're out on the case, have a look for an old piece of furniture. I think this key fits it, maybe a wardrobe, or an old chest of drawers," I hesitated, not sure how to finish my message. "It's Jane," I added, in case it wasn't immediately obvious by my number or my message.

Re-reading the message I'd received with the key; I wondered who my allies could be. I clearly needed local knowledge if I was to solve the mystery. It appeared that while Florence and Marigold would likely know the members of the coven, I wouldn't be receiving any assistance from them. I didn't know Constance or Gwennie well, and I hesitated to contact them after my weird experience with Marigold.

"Just because someone sent me the key, it doesn't necessarily mean they're an ally." Sprinkles wagged his tail as I dropped a couple of pieces of ham in his bowl. Cinnamon watched from her cushion. She didn't require an ongoing supply of food, as did her canine partner. "I'm happy to work alone to solve this, with Ned's help of course," I told her.

My stomach tied itself in too many knots to eat. My brain swirled too much to sleep. Any more coffee and my energy would explode out through my fingers and cause damage, albeit minor, in my cottage. I drew in a deep breath, exhaling as I moved my arms in a circle, directing my energy out through the open windows where it'd dissipate into the air.

Most of my adult life involved me switching between fight and flight mode. Learning a little about my magic, and that others had similar powers, made life a little easier. Focusing on work, in Scotland, and elsewhere helped. I learnt to manage my energy enough to stop outbursts. While my brain wouldn't make sense of anything, I decided to read. At some stage through the pages of my book I fell asleep and dreamt of chasing unicorns and witches on broomsticks. Hooded figures chased me, but I zapped them with fire, and ended up walking through the back of an old wardrobe, with Ned at my side.

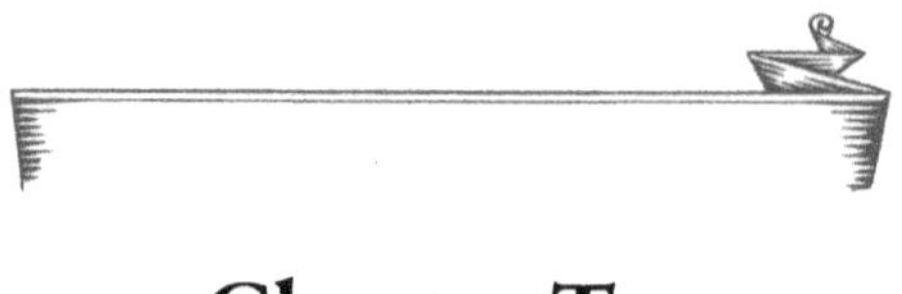

Chapter Ten

As the daylight peeped through my curtains I finally gave in and got out of bed. I groaned as I glanced at the clock. 4:30am was my normal wake up time, but as most of my night had been restless with weird dreams, I didn't feel rested. Sprinkles and Cinnamon followed me to the kitchen, obediently going outside through the pet flap I'd installed. I set up their food and made a coffee as I pondered my next move. I checked my mobile, a little surprised I hadn't heard from Ned. "I hope there were no new developments overnight," I told Bert as I freshened up his water and seed. He chirped his agreement.

"Okay Sprinkles, I'll get into some walking clothes, and we can have an early look around." His tail wagging furiously, he followed me around, standing still while I attached the harness and lead. Ensuring my door key was in my pocket, I closed my front door tightly, still a little shaken by the events of the previous day.

Early morning bird song greeted me as little blue jays and wag tails warbled. Dogs barked in backyards somewhere as they said good morning to whoever was jogging by. Cars moving amiably along the quiet streets. "I love this time of day," I told Sprinkles as he nosed along, checking out each blade of grass, twig, and leaf along the path. I nodded good morning to the other early risers who were taking advantage of the time to fit exercise into their schedule. Misty Vale inhabitants were welcoming people, I felt at home from the first day I stepped off the coach into the main street. It was only as I asked those uncomfortable questions, that I felt a sense that there was a hidden layer of secrecy to this place. "All towns are the same I guess," Sprinkles looked up in agreement, before returning his nose to just above ground level, sniffing the scents known only to him.

I sensed the car before I heard it, my senses on alert after the events of the previous evening. The little dark blue hatch, Ned's personal car, pulled up beside me. "Sorry I didn't get back to you last night, we didn't finish until late. I planned to ring when I got to the station," Ned jumped out of his car to greet me. "Can I give you a lift, or better still, let me buy you a cup of tea as a thank you for the food yesterday. Sophie and I appreciated being able to snack between house calls."

"A tea would be nice. Can Sprinkles ride along in the back? He's well trained."

"Yes, that's fine, he'll smell the scent of my dog though, so as long as he's happy with that," Ned opened the back and I lifted my pup into the space, set up for a similar sized dog, with a bed, lead, water bowl and chew toy. Ned opened a tub, relocating the loose items lest his dog get upset another canine drooled on them.

I stepped into the front seat; glad I hadn't chosen my baggiest gardening tracksuit for my early morning walk. "A lot happened after you left my place last night Ned, but before I fill you in, are you able to tell me anything about the break ins? What items were stolen?" I asked hopefully, not expecting that he'd be able to share many details.

"The victims were reluctant to provide specifics as to what the thief took, if items were taken," Ned's hands gripped the wheel, his voice steady, tired, but determined. "They expect the police to be mind readers," He glanced at me, before turning back to the road in front of us. In a softer voice he asked, "What did you want to tell me?"

I ran the sequence of events from the night before through my head. I decided full disclosure was the best option. "I was at the warehouse, just before the second fire started. Marigold took me there, although I thought we were going somewhere else. I'm not sure she started the fire, though she acted very strangely. You'll find remnants of elemental magic involved, fire, earth, and water. The warehouse collapsed on itself before the water flooded it. I haven't spoken to Marigold since, she drove off as if in a trance," I took a quick breath in, exhaling slowly. "There's a property at 23 North Street, that may be the home of a modern-day coven, as weird as that sounds. I was given a piece of paper with the address on it, after I asked about covens..."

"I know that address, but I don't think it's a coven. Still be careful if you go investigating by yourself. Tell me more about the key," Ned prompted, as he pulled his car in behind the police station.

"I remembered a wardrobe in my family home. I used a similar key to open it. Did you find a piece of old wooden furniture at any of the crime scenes?"

Ned reached into the back seat and pulled out a box of doggy treats. He leant through to where Sprinkles sat, his tongue hanging out, waggling his tail. "Yes. At all five crime scenes in fact. The victims shrugged them off as old, only of sentimental, family value. None produced keys so we could open them. I didn't push it, without any evidence, but I think it's worth looking into further. I don't like coincidences." He patted Sprinkles, who tried to jump out of the back into his arms. "Let's grab a cuppa and we can talk in detail, I want to hear more about that warehouse."

The Milky Bar was open, Jess smiled as we walked through the café doors. "Hello Ned, your usual takeaway, or are you eating in this morning? And Jane, hello, you're earlier than normal."

"I'd no idea you opened this early, and that's dangerous knowledge, as now I know I can get a mocha and a cake during my morning walk," I smiled.

"I'm here early baking, so I may as well open, and catch the early morning customers," Jess grinned. "May I tempt you both with a warm cinnamon scroll?"

"Yes please," I responded, Ned nodded, his mobile to his ear, listening to whoever had just called him. I choose a table near the door while

Ned finished his call. "I'm sorry Jane, but I'm going to have to run. Do you want me to drop your dog over your fence on the way?"

"You'd be going out in a police car? I don't want to make you late. I'll come and get him now," I turned to Jess. "I need to rescue my dog from the police station, can I pick those up to go as well?"

Jess handed Ned his coffee and a couple of bags of baked goods. "We've got a table and chairs outside. You're welcome to sit there with your pup and your cuppa. I'll bring them out when you bring him back."

"Thanks Jess," I'd been looking forward to chatting to Ned, but a mocha and a cinnamon scroll before heading home was acceptable. I made a mental note to include some fruit and vegetables into a meal at some point during the day.

Sprinkles almost jumped into Ned's arms as he opened the back door of his car. "I'm sorry about this Jane. I do want to hear about last night. Can I drop in at your place when I get a chance? Unless I get called out to more incidents."

I grabbed Sprinkles leash before he could run up the street. "Thanks for the lift, Ned. You're welcome to call in anytime," I looked forward to being able to stare into his dreamy brown eyes again soon. "Question before you go, those burglaries, I don't suppose you know if all the homeowners possess some kind of magical ability?"

"All of them. I wish I could give you more information, but if you check out the archives at the library, you should be able to fill in the gaps. I'll catch up with you later."

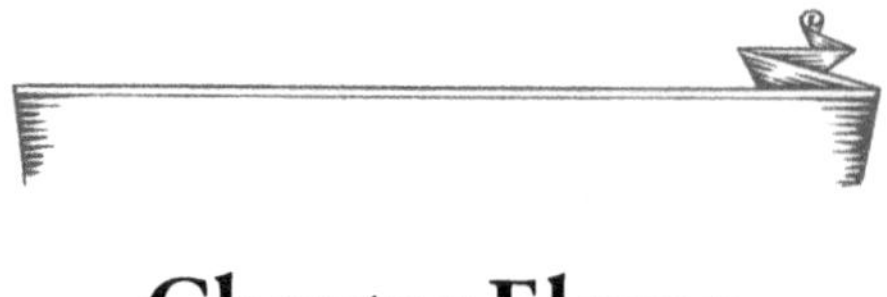

Chapter Eleven

I sipped my mocha, savouring the bitter, chocolatey taste. Sprinkles sniffed the concrete around the table legs, routing out crumbs left behind from other cakes, sandwiches, and baked goods. I saw Florence approaching and had enough time to steel myself before she pounced. "Jane, there you are! I'm so glad I ran into you, though I'd no idea you were up and about so early in the morning," she bent to pat my pup. "What an adorable pup, so well behaved." I wasn't fooled by the fake smile plastered on her face. I'd never noticed before how much of an act she put on. But then, until last night I'd no reason to think anything at all about her, or the others in book club. Were they all members of the coven, and had they orchestrated the fires and the collapse of the warehouse?

"Florence, good morning. Sprinkles and I are often out for an early morning walk. It's generally quiet and peaceful," I hoped she couldn't hear my heart thumping. I wasn't scared of her, but my sixth sense was running on adrenaline. If I unleashed my magic, I'd probably win in a fight against her, but I wasn't keen on finding out.

"I've got some errands to run, but I may call in later this afternoon, for a cuppa and a chat, if you're free," she flashed a passive aggressive smile my way. Sprinkles cocked his head to one side, staring at our visitor, his tail no longer wagging.

I stood so I stared straight into her eyes, rather than looking up, from a seated position. "If I'm home, you're welcome to visit," I kept my voice even, as I picked up my mug and my plate, ready to return it to Jess. Florence's discomfort was evident, clearly not used to being dismissed as she tried to take charge of a situation.

Jess met me at the door. "Thanks," she smiled, as she took my empty crockery. In a softer voice she added conspiratorially, "I couldn't hear what that you ladies said, but not many can say no to Florence and not bear some wrath as a result. I can read body language and believe me, she wasn't happy."

"Let's just say if I stop receiving invitations to book club I won't be surprised," I grinned, an idea forming in my mind, as Sprinkles jumped at Jess. Before I could admonish him, she put the plates down and crouched to pat him. "On a totally different topic," I said before I thought the better of it, "Do you know if Misty Vale has any practising old fashioned witchy covens?"

Jess straightened her knees, picking up the plate and mug before Sprinkles licked them. "Are you looking to join one?" She asked.

"Goodness, no!" I cringed at the idea of being that close to so much magic in one place. "I'm still new to Misty Vale, and curious. I'm not even sure if covens are real. Seeing as some of our village's residents possess magical abilities, I wondered if any groups met to practice spells and crafts..." My voice trailed off as I realised it sounded like I wanted to learn spells from a witch, which was absolutely not what I intended.

Eyeing me warily, Jess shrugged, "Town gossip and all that, there are places where those who are interested meet and practice. Teaching and learning spells if that's your thing. I personally don't like the idea; there's always someone who joins for the wrong reason and ruins it for others." A couple of people walked up to where we were standing in the door. Jess smiled and moved to one side to let them through.

"Thanks," I called after Jess, kicking myself for the way I'd asked about covens. I led Sprinkles along the footpath, aiming for home. We'd been away far longer than I'd planned and although I didn't have any specific tasks for the day, I needed the peace and comfort of home to recharge, at least for a while.

I let Sprinkles set the pace, as we passed shops, and people on their way to work, or school drop off. "So where was Florence going so early this morning?" I wondered aloud, "I don't take her for an early morning exercise person." Sprinkles stopped sniffing the path, staring at me to see if I was talking to him. I'd never owned a dog before he came along, and I was quickly changing my mind about canines. They weren't that different from cats, not really.

At the end of the street, just before the corner where I turned to head home, was an old, abandoned building, that used to be a bank, a shoe shop, and a bakery, at different times, according to the signs on various parts of its walls and awnings. The double doors were open, and I heard muffled, heated voices coming from inside. "What does she know...and what are we to do about it?" it sounded like Florence, but I couldn't be sure.

A higher pitched squeaky voice added, "We can't stop now, we're so close to getting them to agree, it'll only take a few more...incidents." I squinted through the open doorway, trying to identify the speaker. The light was in the wrong position, I couldn't make out any individuals. I hesitated, but as I didn't want to be discovered standing outside trying to eaves drop. I reluctantly crossed the road.

At that moment, a group of three gingerbread men, the size of small children, bounced around the corner, nearly bumping into me. Sprinkles went crazy, trying to follow them, as they raced towards the café. I grabbed and shortened his lead just in time to stop a storybook character losing a limb. Behind me, a pair of singing snowmen bounced around, driving Sprinkle frantic. He pulled at the lead, leaving me with no choice but to continue along the path, in the opposite direction. Once I calmed my pup I looked back towards the empty shop. The doors were shut. Whether anyone was still inside, I couldn't tell from my position. The gingerbread men and snowmen were congregated at the corner near the police station.

"Is Misty Vale always this way, and I haven't noticed?" Sprinkles didn't answer me, and I decided talking out loud mightn't be a good idea, if I didn't want to look crazy. It seemed to me there were several different issues. The distraction of the book characters to misdirect from the thefts, the possibility of covens in the village, the fire and the collapse of the warehouse. All raising more questions. Why? What were the perpetrators trying to achieve?

Chapter Twelve

I opened my mailbox, half expecting another mysterious package. I exhaled, my shoulders relaxing as no new deliveries waited for me. Ned mentioned the library might provide answers to some of my questions, so as much as I'd prefer to spend the day at home, I made sure my pets had water, that my keys, notebook and pen were in my calico bag and headed out for another walk. I hardly used my car, and even considered selling it, though it didn't take up much room in the garage. As I passed Margot's I made a mental note to check in on her when I returned home.

Cathy opened the door to *The Crafty Owl* as I approached, on my way to the library. "Good morning, Jane. I've a few items on sale if you are interested," her wide smile warmed my heart, reminding me that not all residents were like Florence.

"I'm on my way to the library, so I may call past on my way home. I want to sign up for the next workshop too."

"It's filling up fast, if you come in for a minute I'll add your name now, so you don't miss out." I followed Cathy into the store. "The next workshop is Mason Jar Christmas Craft."

"That's the one I'm interested in, thanks. Before I go, do you have any idea who's bringing the Christmas characters to life? Any whispers, or residents who love making Christmas craft?" My voice sounded on edge, I tried to sound lighter, less like I was interrogating my friend. "I mean, I know that's a long shot, but I'm curious as to how they're doing it. Are they creating the creatures from scratch or bringing them to life from books or videos?" My breath caught in my throat. I forced myself to swallow and breathe normally.

"Great minds must think alike Jane, I've been wondering the same thing. Misty Vale is different from everywhere else I've lived. I don't fully understand how everyone's abilities work. I've got no mystical skills, though I can craft up a storm," Cathy grinned. "I'd love magical abilities, but I enjoy what I do, and I love that I can teach what I know to others." She pointed to the table in front of me. "All these sets are fifty percent off for today. Not that you have to buy anything. I've grabbed one of those candle making kits. The resin and lip balm making sets are pretty good too."

"You've sold me on all three, I definitely want to try my hand at those activities. Can you put one of each of those to one side and I'll pick them up on my way home?"

"I sure can," she tucked three boxes under the counter. 'If I figure out how those characters are coming to life, I'll let you know."

"I'll do the same, though I'm not sure I'll be able to figure it out. You interact with many more people during the day than I do. When I ask questions, it always feels like I'm interrogating them," I grinned. "I'll pick them up on the way home from the library." My energy felt lighter after my conversation with Cathy. It restored my faith in the inhabitants of Misty Vale. Not everyone had hidden agendas.

The library building sat on the corner, next to the council chambers. Both were red brick buildings built in the early seventies. On my first visit I read the plaque informing me the interior had received renovations a few years ago, adding a new spacious room with large windows, for clients to sit in the warm sun and read. The microfiche and town history section, located in the older part of the building, contained an impressive array of files, books, and newspaper cuttings.

Kelly, the head librarian and cat lover, who I'd met on my first visit to the vet with Cinnamon and Sprinkles, just after I moved into town, greeted me with a smile.

"I'm heading to the archives, to read up on the town's history. Is the microfiche easy to use?"

"It's easy once you know how. I'm happy to show you how to use it. I have a few minutes before families start coming in for story time." Kelly stepped out from behind the counter. "Are you researching anything in particular?"

"I'm curious about a lot of things. What skills a person would need to be able to bring book and movie characters to life? And more about the magical abilities of our residents. Does their skills run in the family?" I shrugged. "I've lived a lot of places, and I always like to get a feel for the history of the town where I'm living."

The librarian furrowed her brows together. "We don't get many people asking about that sort of thing. Most of us just…I don't know…ignore what's going on around us or take it for granted. Maybe we're just used to it, or it doesn't interest us anymore. Good on you for being inquisitive," she pulled out the metal chair that sat in front of the microfiche machine. "If you sit, I'll show you how to scroll through the reels. We've a lot of material about the founding families, the Wilsons, Elliots, Deans, Murphys, and Devlins. Try those names first. Then pop over to the shelf that houses a couple of books on the history of our village." Kelly pointed to a shelf a few metres away.

A few minutes later I'd figured out the basics of finding newspapers editions and scrolled through the articles relating to unusual or magical events in town. The library records went back over a hundred years, which was more than enough for me. I stood, stretched, and took a long drink of water, grateful I'd remembered to grab my green metal water bottle when I returned to the house. I scanned the pages of notes I'd written. Useful, interesting, but I was no closer to working out what was going on now.

I headed to the shelf Kelly indicated earlier. I flicked through the few books on the history of Misty Vale. Apart from sheep farming, stone fruits, and the broom factory, our village industries included wool and textiles. The annual show featured in a couple of books. Over the years the craft and cooking section created quite a stir with the variety and skill demonstrated by the entrants. The names Kelly mentioned featured in most of the books. I paused my scribbled note taking as my mobile buzzed and vibrated on the table. I rubbed my eyes to clear the fuzziness as I tried to focus on the message from Ned. *Dropped by but you weren't home, will try again later.* Damn. I looked forward to spending time with our local policeman.

My body ached to move, having been hunched over pages for so long. My phone told me it was only 11am but as I'd been awake most of the night, it felt a lot later in the day. I needed a nourishing meal and more water. I drained the last of the liquid from my bottle and returned the books to their shelf. Kelly was showing a customer to the crime section, I caught her eye and waved as I left the library.

A crowd of people stood around the roundabout at the other end of the street. Cars were pulled over to one side, their drivers stood bedside open doors scratching their heads. As I drew closer to the scene, the cause of the ruckus became evident. A giant glittery Christmas tree, at least ten metres tall stood in the middle of the roundabout. Decorated with baubles, lights, and stars with an angel sitting on the top. Shop owners and customers huddled at open shop doors were whispering to each other. I overheard snippets as I walked towards the giant tree. "Where'd the tree come from...It wasn't there an hour ago...Magic or are the council teams getting quicker?"

More misdirection, or an innocent act of Christmas cheer and goodwill? I couldn't be sure. It would have taken hours, if not days to erect the tree using non magical means. Apart from distracting motorists I couldn't see a problem with the festive decoration, but then giggling gingerbread people and singing snowman weren't dangerous either, were they? I turned toward the café, determined to eat something healthier than a cinnamon scroll or a cupcake.

"Welcome back Jane," Jess greeted me with a smile. "Twice in one day. Would you like to try a chicken salad wrap? It's our lunch special."

"That's perfect! I've been at the library all morning and I came out in search of lunch, and some of your freshly made apple juice please."

"Coming right up. You're here at the right time. It's quiet now, but the midday crowd will be here soon. Grab a seat and I'll bring it over." Jess's comment made me curious. As far as I knew she didn't have a helper, so how did she manage customers and meals during the busy time? If I had to guess I'd say elemental magic, and maybe her mum helped out in the kitchen during the lunch rush.

The bell above the door jangled as a couple of well-dressed women entered the café. Both wore navy dresses and heels, with black laptop bags slung over their shoulders. "If the right people sell to us, we'll make a bucket of money marketing this as a popular tourist destination for city folk. If they're curious enough they'll spend their money in Misty Vale," the blonde woman's voice carried across the space.

"Those families have been here for years; they'll not sell easily. We'll have to make it worth their while," responded the brunette.

Chapter Thirteen

I touched my forehead as the familiar thumping, a telltale sign of an impending headache, started. Did the women not care that people around them could hear their discussion? I doubted that residents of Misty Vale would be happy to hand their town over to become a tourist destination. I heard the women order black coffees and cinnamon scrolls. They sat at the table next to mine. I opened my notebook, pretending to read over my morning's work, hoping they'd continue their discussion.

Jess hurried to the table with my order, as the bell signalled more customers. I'd have loved to chat, but she had customers, and I wanted to hear what was being said at the next table.

"The one family who contacted me indicated the others might sell at the right price," the blonde continued their conversation. "We only need five to make it work. The boss has a backup plan, something to do with a key, she said not to worry, it's under control. Did you hear the people on the way here, talking about how the tree just appeared instantly? That's exactly the type of drawcard this place needs to bring the tourists. It's a shame we didn't video it." Both women's hair were tied back into severe pony tails, adding to the sense that both meant business; I just couldn't quite figure out what exactly they were talking about.

The brunette scanned her laptop screen. "If we drive the people in town away, with all these tricks, there won't be much for visitors to see. We don't want those with magic skills to be put out. Don't get me wrong, I want this to work, but we need to realistic. It might take longer than we planned."

"The boss isn't worried about that. People come and go all the time. She said people with magic abilities are drawn here. We know that too, even though some of us try to get as far away as possible, we always return. She promised us lots of money so we can go anywhere in the world, once we finish this." At that point in their conversation, Jess arrived with their order. They ate their scrolls in silence, until Blondie's mobile beeped. "Yes. I understand," she put my mobile on the table. "There's a problem. The boss can't find the key. We must go, now." I continued to eat my chicken wrap, intrigued by the notes I'd taken as the women packed up and brushed past me. I shivered. Something about their energy was more exhausting than most people.

As I scanned the café, most of the tables were occupied, the customers talking about how the Christmas tree arrived without anyone noticing it. "Out of nowhere...Old magic...Elemental magic..." I quickly finished the rest of my lunch, waved goodbye to Jess, and left the café.

There were a few customers lined up at the counter, their arms piled with glitter, tinsel, baubles and Christmas fabric as I ducked into *The Crafty Owl* to pick up my craft kits. After a few minutes it was my turn. "Giant Christmas trees are good for business," I commented with a grin as Cathy served me.

"Yes, that and the annual Christmas decorations competition. Entries will be judged in three weeks. While we aren't supposed to use magic in our creations, some residents will find a way to stretch that definition and create some interesting interpretations," Cathy slipped the craft sets into a brown paper carry bag.

"Maybe that's what's happening with the gingerbread people and snowmen we are seeing wandering around? Someone practising for the competition," I mused aloud.

"It would have to be someone who didn't know the judges won't tolerate that kind of blatant use of magic," Cathy tucked a little packet of tinsel into the bag for me. "You can never have too much tinsel," she grinned.

An older lady I didn't know, lined up beside me. I wanted to ask about the judges and the details of the competition, but I didn't want to keep the customer waiting. "I'll let you know how I go with these kits."

"Please do," Cathy responded as she scanned the customers balls of wool. "The competitions details are on social media if you're interested in creating an entry."

As I neared home, I walked up the path of the house next door. I wanted to make sure Margot had calmed since the snowman incident. She opened her door before I had a chance to use the antique brass door knocker in the shape of a gargoyle head. "You looked frazzled," she said in that deadpan, no nonsense way that reminded me of my third-grade teacher, Miss Carey.

"It has been a long day," I admitted. "I wanted to check in to see how you were going. After the run in with that snowman."

"Pish, posh. That was days ago. I've not seen hide nor snowball of him since. Are you going to stand there or come in for a cup of tea?" Margot moved to one side to allow me to enter her home. A place I'd the privilege of seeing only a couple of times before. Old school, private and fiercely independent, Margot was, like me, not a fan of fools. "You've had some visitors recently," my neighbour said as she poured tea from her floral teapot into matching cups.

"I'm sorry if Sprinkles has been barking, he gets excited when he sees people." I admired the pale blue floral pattern on my cup, it reminded me of something long forgotten.

Margot leant over to the blue metal biscuit tin, pulling off the lid as she passed it to me. The familiar shaped shortbread biscuits invoked memories of sewing kits we'd used at primary school. A long time ago. "His barking doesn't worry me. From here I can see your gate," she pointed through the side window. "That policeman, a couple of other people I didn't recognise, and that bossy lady, the one who's on every committee."

"Florence Hartly?" I asked, pleased I'd missed that visitor.

"She rushed to your door, full of self-importance and huffed all the way back out again when you didn't answer. That was after that policeman came by," Margot placed a biscuit on her saucer.

I took a bite of the scroll shaped biscuit, enjoying the sugary melt in the mouth sensation on my tongue. "You mentioned I had other visitors?" I prompted, curious as to who else would be knocking on my door.

"I've no idea who they were. I don't know everyone in town."

An idea formed in the recesses of my brain. "You've lived here a long time?"

"Born and bred here. Moved away for a while but returned," Margot raised her cup to her lips.

I drained my tea in one go, trying not to gulp too loudly. "You'd know the important families, those who've been here forever." Margot stared, her eyes squinting to me over the top of her cup. "I guess I want to know more about the town I'm living in, the people and their abilities."

Margot frowned, "You'll want to know about the founding families. Stay clear of them, though it's not easy now they've changed their names."

"Pardon?" My teacup cluttered to its saucer before I could catch it. My fingers shook, for reasons I didn't understand.

"The families, the names listed as those that founded the town, with the ability to manipulate the elements. Most of them changed their names years ago. Something about keeping the town safe, which I think is a load of poppycock. Our town can't be safe if it's based on secrets. But that's just my opinion," she said gruffly.

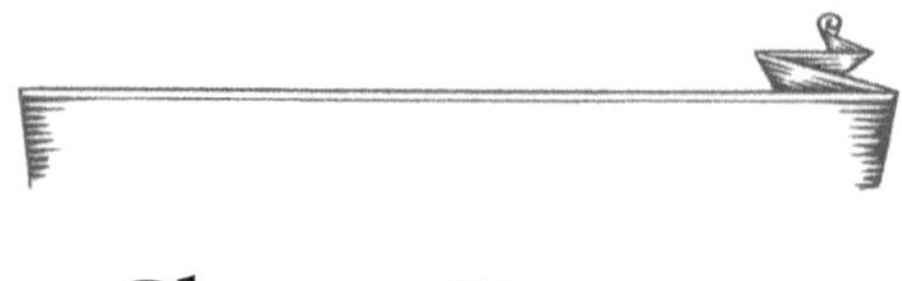

Chapter Fourteen

I looked around Margot's part lounge, part dining room. A door led to her kitchen, another to a hallway. Our cottages were similar in layout; I wondered if they'd been built by the same person. Unlike my eclectic undefined colour scheme, my neighbour's décor was predominantly blue. The curtains, the cushions on the dining chairs and the lounge, the rug on the floor, all shades of that pretty blue, darker than light, but not navy. The furniture in the room looked old, antique. Did Margot herself come from money? Could she belong to one of the original Misty Vale families?

Margot's shoulders slumped a little, then she drew herself up in her seat. "I do belong to one of those families as it happens. I'm not proud of it, and I don't associate with any of them. Before you ask, yes, I know who they are, and their skills. I still have all my marbles, just no time for games and drama."

"Why did you come back, if you prefer to stay away from your family and friends?" My fingers tapped on the table as I tried to control my emotions. Could it be my neighbour had the answers I was looking for? Why did I suddenly feel so invested in this? Finding the key and note, someone obviously thought I'd a role to play. "Actually, don't answer that, it wasn't fair of me to ask. I can be too nosy, I forget I'm no longer employed as a police person, or a private eye. Do you know if there's any significance to an old metal key, or a piece of furniture it may open?"

Margot stood and cleared away the cups, saucers and teapot. I couldn't read her expression, but she appeared conflicted. I let her mutter to herself, intrigued as to what she'd say next. My sixth sense told me she understood my question about the key. "We all have one. The key and a wardrobe or chest of drawers it unlocks. Part of our family heritage. A load of rubbish, as far as I'm concerned, but still…" I waited for Margot to think through what secrets she might be about to reveal. "Why do you ask about a key?"

I considered how to respond. I didn't have any reason not to believe my neighbour, or not to trust her. "Someone left an old key and a note in my mailbox yesterday. The note implied I was the key to something important. I don't know what they're referring to, or what the key opens. There's been so much going on around the village in the last few days. Giant book characters coming to life, fires, the river turned to lemonade, thefts, now a giant Christmas tree, and who knows what else."

"Part of that is easy to solve, when you've lived here as long as I have," Margot returned to the table and sat opposite me. "The characters coming to life, will be old Mr and Mrs Kenny. They used to teach at the local school, and they've written a few children's books. They don't belong to one of the original families, but they love bringing characters to life. They've been travelling for the last couple of years and returned home just before Halloween. I didn't know they were back when snowy arrived in my backyard. I ran into them yesterday. They didn't say they were the creators of the lively characters, but it wouldn't surprise me if they were," Margot's voice softened, her eyes sparkled, I could tell she thought highly of the teachers. "Or maybe one of their former students. I heard stories that a gang of youth, who discover the Kenny's secret and brought a whole heap of cartoons to life. Scared the heck out of the people who ran into them. Years ago," she stared through the open curtains into the yard. Her eyes glazed, wrapped in memories of times past.

Not sure how to respond, I kept quiet, watching my neighbour, to see if she'd reveal additional information. I eyed the biscuit tin, though

I didn't feel like any more biscuits. Too many sweet things and my stomach flip flopped. I craved some of the fresh grapes I knew were sitting in my fridge next door.

"I suppose it could all be misdirection," she mused. "You said something about houses being broken into. What better way to distract the local law enforcement than setting them on wild gingerbread and snowmen chases?"

"That's exactly what I thought, though I don't know how it's all linked." I placed the lid back on the biscuit tin and handed it to Margot. "Do you know if any covens meet locally? Or who lives at 23 North Street?" I asked, remembering the strange events involving Marigold.

"Too many questions will get you killed girlie," Margot's tone changed suddenly. "You'd better go," she pointed to her front door. I grabbed my bag off the floor as she ushered me out. "And keep that dog of yours quiet," she barked as she shut her door firmly behind me.

My pup jumped up and down at the gate in greeting, tail wagging and tongue hanging out. "Hi Sprinkles, that was a strange visit with Margot," I patted him with one hand, while I rummaged around for my key with my other. A prickling across the back of my neck, alerted me that I wasn't alone. Did Margot sense something sinister, the reason behind the change in her attitude towards me?

"Let me help you with that." I jumped as Ned appeared behind me, picking up the paper bag of goodies from the craft shop.

Certain it wasn't his presence that had my spider senses on alert, I took the opportunity to gaze beyond the fence as I smiled at him. "That'd be great, thanks," I caught a flash, a movement across the road. Not enough detail to pick up who'd been spying, but my intuition told me I knew the person. "Have you got time for a cuppa?" I didn't feel like more tea or coffee, but I yearned for a big glass of water.

Ned pushed the door open navigating the pup and cat both vying for our attention. "Just to sit a while would be welcome, if it comes with caffeine, even better," Ned sounded as tired as I felt as he slid into one of my kitchen chairs.

I filled two large purple glasses of water and added a couple of ice cubes. I placed one in front of Ned. "Tea? Coffee?" I asked as I filled the kettle.

"Coffee please, and thanks for the water. You had something to tell me this morning?" Ned drank half the glass in one gulp.

Our meeting earlier in the day seemed like a lifetime ago. I did have things to tell Ned, even more details than before. "I'm sure this is going to make me sound crazy," was how I began, "Marigold Sparks and I were at the warehouse last night, when the fire started. I saw a wave of water from the river wash over the building; but before that, the earth shook so much the building collapsed." I paused, knowing that even for Misty Vale this sounded odd.

Ned looked up from his notepad, where he'd been scribbling notes as I spoke. "We came up with evidence of elemental magic as the cause of the incident at the warehouse. The problem with this is that elemental magic is extremely difficult to prove. Also, whose magic is an even bigger question. Unfortunately, the residue magic doesn't leave a signature pointing us to the culprit," he sighed. "I take it that's not all."

"Not even close. Do you know for sure if there are covens in Misty Vale?"

Ned nodded. "We have evidence of covens. Don't think of them as the evil witch gatherings of stories and movies. Covens in Misty Vale are harmless, people getting together to practice some of their skills, or maybe teach each other, informally."

"When you describe it like that, it sounds like any other group of people who meet to discuss things they have in common. There's something about Marigold and Florence," I considered my next words while I poured water into two mugs. Coffee for Ned and peppermint tea for me. I placed both mugs on the table. "I don't trust them, they're keeping secrets. Not that they have to tell me stuff, just because I ask," I slid the metal key over to Ned. "Then there's this key, it's important somehow. The note that came with it tells me I am part of the solution to the mystery, which makes no sense." I picked up the metal key, turning it over in the palm of my hand. "I know from Margot, next door, that the members of the founding families, own a piece of furniture that this key, or one like it, will fit," I sipped my cup of herbal tea, allowing the scent of peppermint to permeate my senses. This herb, more than any others, energised me, awakening my energy, my magic.

"Do you think that your key would unlock the furniture belonging to those families?" Ned looked up hopefully. "Why though? I wonder what the significance is of the furniture of what's inside them?"

"I have no idea. Maybe nothing at all, and whoever left it for me is trying to distract me from figuring out what's going on," I took another quick sip from my mug, letting the herbal tea calm my emotions. I needed logic to figure out the mystery. "I was at the café, for something to eat, after spending the morning at the library. I overheard a couple of women talking about making our village into a tourist attraction. There was something off about them. They mentioned a 'boss' and moving slowly but getting the families on board," I rubbed my fingers along my forehead. "Sorry, I've been talking so much, probably the last thing you need."

The policeman smiled, a worn smile that nevertheless was genuine. "When I asked you to help, and I had no idea this thing, whatever it is, would have so many moving parts. Not for a minute did I think you'd be targeted by whoever is involved. I don't think you're in danger, exactly, and I believe in your ability to see through the rubbish and sort out what's important," Ned emptied his mug, and his glass of water. "This is a strange case, and I fear we're only at the start of it." He stood up, as his mobile beeped. "Why don't you chill for the rest of the day, and I'll call past first thing in the morning."

"A book or maybe some knitting, does sound more relaxing than this mystery," I acknowledged. It had been a big couple of days. Being around so many people drained me, and time alone would give me a chance to recharge my batteries.

Ned's mobile rang buzzed and beeped. "Sorry, I've got to get this," he picked his phone out of his pocket.

While he listened and asked questions, I cleared the table, stacking the washing up in the sink. Sprinkles stood beside me, staring at me. "Hoping for a snack?" I asked him. His tail wagged, as I grabbed a dog treat from the cupboard.

"I've got to meet Sophie at the next crime scene. A huge snow dump, just outside of town. I've no idea what we can do about it, but we must attend and erect a cordon around the area. Until it all melts and causes more problems," I heard the tiredness in Ned's voice. Being a policeman in a town with this much elemental magic would be exhausting at the best of times. I patted the policeman on the shoulder as he headed out through the front door. It seemed appropriate. We hadn't quite shared a moment, but we were both trying to solve the same mystery, which made it a shared bond. "Let's catch up tomorrow and share any updates."

"Sounds good," I agreed. As I closed the door behind him, I had the feeling this was just the start of the mystery of Misty Vale.

Chapter Fifteen

As I rolled the rainbow-coloured plastic ball for Cinnamon and Sprinkles a thought, half formed, and elusively played around the edge of my mind. Margot mentioned the families had changed their names, but I'd not asked why, or what their new names were. I didn't feel like asking Margot more questions. Maybe I'd text Ned and ask him the names of the victims of the break ins, so I could cross reference the names.

Sprinkles nosed the ball under the coffee table. Cinnamon crouched, waiting for it to roll out the other end. It didn't. Using the table for support I got to my knees, to see what was blocking the balls path.

What the?

A wooden box I'd not seen before sat under the table, preventing the ball from travelling to the other side. About the same size as my cardboard box, I extricated the plain pine box, pushing the ball through to my cat, who waited patiently at the other end. She batted it back to Sprinkles, and their game continued.

Odder than finding a box I'd not seen before under my table, was the absence of any dust on the top of it. If it'd been there any length of time it should show signs of dust, and animal fur. Both my pets were known for moulting, a truth that drove me to distraction most days. "I wish I knew more about magic. Could a person have magicked this here, or did they have to break in to leave it?" I asked aloud as I held out the box to Sprinkles who sniffed it and went back to chasing the ball. What reaction had I expected? A growl maybe, if an intruder had broken in and dropped it under there.

Can you swing past when you get a chance please? I messaged Ned, as I sat in my chair, trying to calm the nervous energy running throughout my body before opening the box. A knock at the door a few minutes later pulled me to my feet. "That was quick," I opened the door, expecting to see the policeman.

Florence's fake smile greeted me. "I did call in a couple of times earlier, but you weren't home. Your lovely pup here greeted me at the gate."

Could Florence be the person who delivered the package, or the key? It didn't feel like something she'd do. She operated through purely selfish motivation, while trying to appear generous. "Florence. It's nice to see you," I hoped she couldn't read auras, or she'd know I wasn't particularly pleased at all.

"I hope you don't mind, but I'd love a cup of tea. I've been running errands all day," she pushed past me, with the expertise and self-assurance of someone always used to getting her own way.

I stepped gently in front of her and led her to the kitchen. I knew a thing or two about working with passive aggressive personalities; I quietly shifted the balance of power. "I'm a little busy myself, though I do have time to spare for a quick cuppa ." I motioned to the seat Ned vacated, watching my second visitor as I gathered the tea bags and clean mugs. Normally Sprinkles would be all over any visitor, and I'd find myself apologising for his boisterous behaviour. Interestingly, neither animal were paying any attention to Florence.

"I sensed you wanted to ask more questions yesterday, before we received news of the fire," Florence's tone reminded of that snake cartoon character from my childhood. The one that sounded friendly and welcoming, but I should treat with a healthy dose of caution. "Our little village isn't mysterious at all. Sure, there are folk with special abilities, but there's nothing sinister or untoward here. Covens aren't really a thing. People meet to talk about their skills, like the CWA meet to exchange recipes or the church or charities meet up. I hope that eases any concerns you have."

It sounded like well-rehearsed misdirection to me. "Of course. I understand exactly what you've said. I know there's no evil intent in our beautiful village, that the cute creatures popping up all over town are harmless Christmas gifts for the villagers. I'm so pleased I fell in love with the town and decided to stay," I used my own ability to read people, to gauge her reactions to my words. A skill I honed through years of investigative work, assessing potential suspects, or sources of danger. Her aura gave her away, relieved that I seemed to buy her story, yet worried I'd keep asking questions. I decided not to mention I'd been reading up on Misty Vale's history.

"I fear you may have witnessed some strange behaviour from Marigold last night," Florence's voice sounded cordial, but strained. "I must apologise for my friend; she'd taken a double dose of her medication yesterday. Forgetting she'd already taken her tablet, she took a second one with breakfast and hallucinated for most of the day, poor thing. I hope she didn't cause you any alarm."

"Oh no. I hope she'll be okay." Whether or not what Florence said had any truth to it, which I doubted, I decided to play down the events and see how she reacted. "After she took me to the warehouse she vanished. When I couldn't find her, I headed home. Apart from wondering where she went, there was no harm done."

The relief that flooded through my visitor plainly evident as a wave; she physically relaxed her body in front of me, "She'll be fine. I have her at my place, so I can look after her. Gwennie and Constance are there while I've been running errands. I'm pleased to hear she didn't scare or upset you," Florence lifted her mug, drinking most of the hot liquid in one gulp. Her body jumped, ever so slightly. I followed her gaze to where the key sat on the table. Composing herself, she wiped her top lip with her thumb, as if wiping stray drops of tea away. "That's an interesting key."

A few scenarios ran quickly through my mind. If I said I found it, she'd likely offer to take it to find its owner, seeing as she knew most people in town. If I said it was given to me, she'd want to know why. For reasons that weren't entirely clear, I went with – "It was my grandmothers. She gave it to me before she passed away. It's her birthday today and I always feel close to her when I have the key with me. I'm considering making into a piece of jewellery or a centrepiece for my mantel."

Florence's eyebrows raised, ever so slightly. I may have imagined the quiver in her voice as she asked, "May I touch it? I love old pieces like this."

I nodded, with no idea why I felt reluctant to let my visitor handle the key. It wasn't as if it were a family heirloom with emotion attached to it. I never knew any of my grandparents, or where my parents came from. Whenever I asked, they quickly changed the subject. My story could well have been true. Inexplicably, hot tears welled in the corner of my eyes. I couldn't think of an excuse to forbid her to touch it. "Go ahead," Maybe she'd comment that she'd seen keys like it or ask if my grandmother's key opened a piece of antique furniture. She didn't.

"It is a lovely way of remembering your grandmother," she said at last, as an expression I couldn't quite place flited across her countenance.

"Keys, and the furniture they unlocked, were made to last, back in the olden days," I couldn't help baiting her, to see if Florence accidentally revealed any information. It couldn't be a secret, that other families in Misty Vale owned antique keys that opened old items of furniture. "I wish I could remember what this opened. Does Misty Vale have a second-hand shop? Wouldn't it be marvellous I found an old wardrobe that opened with this key? I'll keep an eye on the for-sale ads in case such a piece comes up," I smiled, excited at the prospect, and pleased I'd riled Florence. For reasons I didn't fully understand, seeing her uncomfortable made me happy. Probably the way she bossed other people around. I know her attitude irked me.

I noticed her flinch, such a slight movement, as if she'd been bitten by a nasty ant. "You could try dear, but I don't think the owners of such an item would easily part with it. If I think of anyone who may want to sell one, I'll be sure to let you know." she replied, her false smile firmly plastered on her face. Slowly, Florence pushed her chair back and rose to her full height. She sucked in a mouthful of air and stuck her chest out, an old intimidation trick of bullies worldwide. "Thanks for the tea. I really must dash; I want to see how poor Marigold is faring."

Quick as a flash I moved so I blocked her exit. Two could play at the power games. "Thanks so much for dropping by. Please give her my best wishes for a speedy recovery."

"I will. She'll be pleased to hear you bear no hard feelings; she was embarrassed by her behaviour. Florence stepped to one side as Cinnamon pounced just to her right. My pets were giving off unusual unwelcoming vibes. Animals were great judges of character.

I pulled open my door for the second time in less than an hour, to release Florence from my stalking cat, just as Ned walked through the front gate. Sprinkles ran past Florence and jumped up at Ned, waggling his tail, clearly excited at our visitor. "Ned thanks for calling in. I have some more slice ready for you and Sophie, it's inside in a container ready to go. I didn't like the idea of it going to waste. The kettles not long been boiled so if you have a minute we can compare crosswords."

Ned easily followed my lead, "Thanks Jane, you're a lifesaver, that slice is amazing melt in your mouth awesomeness. Crossword number 568 is a little tricky, there are some tough codes to crack in that one. Good afternoon, Mrs Hartly."

Florence looked from Ned to me and back. "Good afternoon," she looked like she wanted to say more but thought the better of it and quickly passed through the gate, the metal lock banging in place behind her.

Chapter Sixteen

Ned followed me inside. "I fear you'd be a formidable crossword opponent, chess, or poker too. I hope you do have some more of that slice for us."

I smiled, "I do, as it happens. I'll swap you some slice for information if you have time and I've another mystery to solve."

"I thought you were going to take it easy for the rest of the day?" Ned raised his eyebrows as he followed me to the kitchen.

"So did I," I checked the water level in the kettle and switched it on to boil. "Are you able to tell me the names of those who reported break ins? And what do you know about those important families in Misty Vale changing their names?" While I waited for the kettle, I rescued the pine box from where it was hidden in plain sight on my comfy chair. Florence hadn't reacted when she glanced at it on the way to the front door. I placed it on the table in front of my friend. "I found this under the coffee table, just before I messaged you. I've not seen it before, and it wasn't covered in dust or animal hair, so it hasn't been there for long. Do you know if it could have been magicked here or whether someone must've broken in to hide it? Both sound implausible, but one scenario must be likely."

The policeman frowned as he turned the box over, examining it. "What's inside?"

I stretched out my palms for the box. "I don't know. Florence arrived before I could open it," I slowly positioned the box on the table between us, not far from the key, which clearly didn't open this much newer smaller mystery. Whatever waited for the old key to unlock its secrets would have to wait a little longer.

The pine wood felt smooth to touch. The brassy clasp was cheap, like the box, wasn't part of a family heirloom. My fat fingers fiddled it, loosening the loop, until it popped from the knob. The lid lifted gradually on its hinges, revealing the contents; a pile of papers folded together, tied with some old brown string, a couple of sepia photographs, and a passport. The woman with the serious face in the passport could have been a relative of mine, or maybe it was a picture of my mother, taken a long time ago. Except the name wasn't Jenny Fairweather, it was Sandra Devlin. I stared at the passport photo, the unsmiling eyes of the woman staring back at me, or rather at the photographer who took the photo.

"You've gone pale, may I see?" My hands shook uncontrollably as I handed the passport over to Ned.

"The woman looks a little like my mother," I offered by way of explanation. I looked at the other photographs, of a family standing around a rather large tree, a Christmas tree judging by the trinkets hung in its branches. Smiling faces posing for the camera, recording what appeared to be a family Christmas. The same woman from the passport was in the photo, as were two women who looked similar, one a little younger and a much older one – the mother perhaps. A man a similar age, with smiling eyes, and two younger versions, the woman's brothers maybe, all smiling at the photographer. Two other photographs similarly recorded family events, a picnic and a piano singalong. Another photo, a slightly different size and colour to the posing family, showed a little boy, sat on the lap of a stern looking woman. Beside her stood a man who looked as if a strong gust of wind would bowl him over. I handed the photographs over for my visitor to see. "Not my mother though, she was an only child."

"What are those?" Ned pointed to the pile of papers. My fingers seemed to have a mind of their own, as I struggled to undo the string that bound the folded papers together. Ned held out his hands to help, but I persisted.

Finally, the papers unfolded in front of me, I read them. "Birth certificates, for Sandra Devlin, Alexander Thorne and Clara Thorne." My breath caught in my throat as I read the birth dates on the documents.

"What is it?" Ned asked.

After re-reading the information a couple of times, I passed the pages over. "Birth certificates of three locals according to the documents. I haven't met them, or even heard of them..." My heart seemed to have a mind if its own, pounding in my chest. "It's their birthdays; the man has the same date and year of birth as my dad, the older woman has the same as my mother, and the younger woman was born the same day and year as I." I really didn't know what to make of what I read.

"To add to the mystery, you asked about the families with the break ins. Thornes, Devlins, and Murphys. Wilsons, Eliotts and Deans. Although, they're not Deans anymore, they changed their family name to Spark about twenty years ago. Some of the Elliots go by the name Gale, and over the generation's others decided to revert back to their mother's maiden names for reasons I haven't figured out," he scratched his head. "Where are your folks from? Where did you grow up?"

"My parents were always difficult to pin down with any family history. Neither had siblings, both grew up in suburbs of Sydney and met at university. My grandparents passed away before I was born. Both my parents are gone now. There's no one left to corroborate their version of my ancestry. I grew up in a big country town. I much prefer the quieter pace of village life."

Ned's phone beeped. He put the papers on the table, taking his mobile out of his shirt pocket. "I've got to go, are you going to be okay?"

I nodded, unable to speak as my mind whirred through so many thoughts; I swallowed, as my stomach clenched, threatening to expel my last meal. I followed Ned to the door. Giving me a look of concern, his eyes a little wider than normal, he turned, reluctant to leave me. I read all that in his face, or was I imagining it? "I'll be fine, I am fine," I managed to squeak out. In a firmer voice I added, "I'll lock the door behind you, and sit and read, or knit, for the rest of the day. You can catch me up on what's happening around town when we meet tomorrow."

The rest of the day passed in a blur as I fed the animals, cleaned the kitchen, scrubbed the bathroom and vacuumed the cottage. Cleaning always helped me process information. Cleaning and running away were my go-to tasks when things got a little hairy. I wasn't planning on leaving my cottage and my pets, not without a fight.

Chapter Seventeen

I woke before the alarm feeling much better. The first rays of light of the new day told me I was out of bed before 5am. Again. Cinnamon and Sprinkles didn't mind, wrapping themselves around my legs as I made my way to the kitchen to feed them, and Bert. I left them crunching and munching and let the hot droplets of water soothe away the confusion and uncertainty of the previous day. *A hot shower and a cup of tea solves everything.* One of my mother's sayings.

It didn't really matter if I didn't know a lot about my parents' past. I knew they loved me and did their best to look after me. My childhood had been happy, and safe. Although the problems I faced as my magic spilt out of control may have been averted had I known more, I couldn't change the past. I decided instead to focus on the present.

My intuition prompted me to ask some questions. I just wasn't sure who to ask them to. *Did I like it here, and choose to settle in this village because it was the place of my ancestors? Is this where my magic came from after all?* Just as importantly – *If all this were true, why would my parents bother to keep this a secret? Could I be related to others in Misty Vale? And who in town figured it all out?* Someone must have, to be sending me a key and a box with papers and photographs for identification.

Hazel Thorne. The name popped into my head as I tied my laces, ready for an early morning walk. "Now where did that name come from?" I asked Sprinkles as he nosed my hand. "Let's go for a walk, clear the cobwebs," I attached his lead and harness to a very excited pup. That he kept still enough for me to do so was a blessing. I wasn't in the mood for the dance that normally followed me trying to put Sprinkle's harness on.

Did I read the name Hazel Thorne in a book once, or is she a character from a movie or television show? Her name stared at me from the birth certificate of the man named Alexander. If this was a record of my father's birth, that would make Hazel my grandmother. "Right Sprinkles let's get out and move. Cinnamon, you and Bert are in charge." My budgie chirped, while my cat continued to lick her paws, a trait which my pup copied on the few occasions he sat still.

Without planning my route, I found myself outside 23 North Street. My feet led me there while my brain tried to work out the stitches required for adapting a knitted pattern for Santa Claus into a snowman. I purposefully refused to think of recent events, until I stood in front of a building that may be home to a coven. *Was Hazel Thorne a witch?* No idea where that question came from. *Were one or both of my parents born to one of the founding families?*

I forced myself to think through how to knit a gingerbread man, rather than trying to puzzle out the scenario I currently found myself in. A trick I used to calm my anxiety – focusing on a logic, solvable problem allowed my brain breathing space to process things rationally. "It's not working Sprinkles," I sighed. He didn't care, having found one of a hundred different scents that intrigued him when we set foot outside. "It's a terrier thing," I smiled, my heart filling with love for my furry friend.

A terrier. I'd been called that before, and *A bull at a gate,* due in a large part to my tenacity, stubbornness and determination. Ned was right, nine and a half times of out ten, when given a mystery I'd solve it. Except when it related to me. "I'm looking at this the wrong way round," I told Sprinkles. "I need to pretend this problem belongs to someone far removed from me and Misty Vale." Solving crimes, puzzles, revealing the guilty, all depended on objectivity. "And coffee, definitely coffee."

With renewed enthusiasm, to view this mystery impartially, I paid attention to the building in front of me. The thick, prickly hedge hid most of the house. In contrast, the plants just beyond the hedge were old fashioned cottage bushes, roses and geraniums as well as an assortment of others I knew only by their brightly coloured petals. The house façade was wooden, not weatherboard, as I originally thought; and when I stood at the right angle, I noticed a black rocking chair, draped with colourful fabric on the front verandah. With my mobile in my hand, I snapped a few photos of what I could see, knowing that once I interrogated the photographs, I'd notice more details. It was a well-loved, well looked after home. Marigold wanted me to visit it. Was I supposed to knock on the door?

My heart jumped into my mouth, at least that's what it felt like, as the gate opened just as I was about to open it. "Can I help you?" A lady, her grey hair plaited and piled high on her head smiled. "I saw you standing out here, are you lost?"

"I'm not sure. I mean, no, I'm not lost exactly. Someone mentioned this address, and I wasn't sure why. I guess I was curious." Did my words make any more sense to this stranger than they made to me?

"Ah I see. Because I'm the local witch no doubt," her eyes twinkled warmly as she spoke. "Pay me no mind dear, a lot of us are witches, at least, many of us can manipulate the elements. Change outcomes and bring items to life. It's not for the faint hearted. Some people run away. I can see you're not one of them. Do you want to come in for a cup of tea? Your pup will be fine as long as he stays clear of Esmerelda." At that moment a dainty grey tabby climbed out of the hedge onto the lady's shoulder. Instead of trying to jump up and chase the cat, as was usual for my dog, he hid behind my leg.

My curiosity piqued, overriding my fear. "That'd be lovely, although I have a meeting later, I can spare half an hour." It wasn't an outright lie, I'd planned to catch Ned at some point throughout the day, visit the library, the craft shop and the café. It was always better to make it ap-

pear like someone would be expecting me, that if I disappeared someone would notice.

Tilting her head slightly with a knowing look that told me I wasn't
fooling her, she ushered me through the gate and up to a little wicker
table settings with two chairs, that I hadn't seen from the path. She motioned for me to sit. The table held a china teapot and matching cups
and saucers. Hand painted dainty pink flowers adorned the crockery.
Purple cushions on the chairs matched the placemats on the table.

The cushion was surprisingly comfortable, as I gingerly placed my
backside onto the chair offered to me. I looped Sprinkles leash around
my arm so he couldn't wander far. The last thing I needed was him to
choose to chase Esmerelda. I needn't have worried, he sat as still as a
mouse as close to my foot as he could be, his head lying on my toes.

"You have so many questions child," The older woman spoke softly.
It was odd, being referred to as a child. I watched in silence as she
poured dark liquid from the teapot into my cup. "My name is Hazel.
You look so much like your mother, though I haven't seen her in over
thirty years." I wasn't as surprised as I should have been. The revelation
that this woman knew my mother, that I may be related to her, an easy
truth to believe. I concentrated on Hazel's face, the sound of her voice
seemed calming to me. Could she hear the thumping of my heart in my
chest? "When they chose to leave it broke my heart, but I understood,
neither of them wanted this life for their child."

I wasn't aware I was crying, until I tasted the salt of my tears on the
corners of my mouth. My mouth opened, but no sound came out, despite the jumble of words in my head.

"When I heard of their passing, I knew you'd arrive. As is the way
of things, the veil lifted for you at the time they passed to the other-
world. Throughout the years and your travels, I watched you struggle
with your skills and wished I could help. It wasn't possible, for I'd made
a vow to them, not to interfere in your life." I saw so many other words
on her face, things she wanted to say. I watched as she struggled with

how much to reveal. Rather than speak, she reached her hand out, covering mine.

My mouth opened, still no words managed to escape. The one word, on a loop that I couldn't get out of my brain – home.

Chapter Eighteen

Finally, Hazel, my grandmother, removed her hand. It felt like an eternity that we'd sat together communicating without words. Somewhere inside the cottage a cuckoo clock told us it was 7am. Following her lead, I sipped my warm tea. It tasted of peppermint, ginger, lemon and a flavour I couldn't place.

"Aniseed," my grandmother read my mind. I smiled at the term of endearment that flashed through my mind, not quite sure I believed that at nearly forty years old, I sat opposite a member of my family. "Yes, child, Jane, or may I call you Clara, you were so small last time I saw you, I can read your mind. You have so many questions. I will answer them all, but not all at once." I couldn't stop staring into Hazel's eyes, as if I averted my gaze, she'd disappear. "Please know that your parents loved you and didn't make their decision without first thinking through so many options. You must understand that back then, Thorne's and Devlin's weren't supposed to wed. Conceiving a child where both parents were spirit elementals was unheard of. You'd have grown up under a microscope with people watching your every move to see what magic you possessed."

My gaze left her eyes. With so much emotion in the air, I didn't know where to look. I focused on the plants around us on the verandah and in the front garden. Lavender, rosemary, roses, geraniums, varieties that were growing in my little garden. "I guess I understand that," I spoke slowly. "I wish they'd told me about their history, my history, their powers, my powers. Misty Vale, where I came from, that I had family here. A grandmother," My face twisted into a smile, despite the tears running down my cheeks. "Weird things have happened around me my whole life. It would've helped if I'd known I wasn't a freak," I shook my head, to clear away the residue melancholy that always accompanied my reminiscing.

"Your parents would've been scared that you'd leave them and return here," Hazel whispered gently.

"I must admit, they'd have probably been correct. I've been running most of my life. This is the first place that's felt like home. I lived overseas for a long time, and living in the bigger cities in Australia, where it was easier to hide. None of the places I've lived have felt like home, until now," I wriggled my toes as Sprinkles stirred. "I've lived in Misty Vale for only a few months..." My heart leapt to my throat as a thought popped into my head. "Did you know I was here?" *And if so, why didn't you reach out*? I added to myself.

The older woman sighed, her whole body shuddered, the depths of sadness as clear as the sunny sky above our heads. "Such was the pact I made with your parents. I promised not to make contact first. I was torn, once they died, and you arrived here. With every fibre of my soul, I wanted to connect with you. Many times, I drove past your cottage, slowing down in case you were outside in your front garden," Tears filled her eyes. Her hand shook as she lifted her cup to her mouth and drank what remained of her tea. "You've been quiet and kept to yourself, apart from book club and I'm not welcome there, but that's another story. I didn't manage to run into you at the café or the craft shop. I was tempted to follow you, but I couldn't bring myself to," Esmerelda appeared from the bushes behind Hazel, daintily walking along her shoulders, before wrapping herself into the woman's lap. Tears fell from Hazel's eyes. I reached out and gently touched my grandmother's arm. Her eyes smiled through her tears as she continued to speak. "I made the first move in the end. Although it was Marigold who gave away my address, poor Mari. I left the key for you, and the documents," Her hands found her feline's back and gently stroked her fur. "I wish I'd been there to guide you through the contents of the box, but that hateful woman turned up. All I could do was hide the box and disappear."

I exhaled, the pent-up energy and angst eased as my grandmother's recounting of events helped me to slot the puzzle pieces in place. I still had hundreds of questions, but not nearly as many as before. "I don't like Florence much either. She bosses and intimidates everyone. I've been avoiding people like that all my life. The last time I saw her, I had her on the back foot," I smiled at the memory.

"I think you're a lot like me. Strong, determined and you don't give up easily. My only regret is I gave you up. That I honoured my promise to your parents. It broke my heart when they left, that I wouldn't be able to help them to teach you our ways or show you how to master our specific magic and energy," She paused, tilting her head a little to her right as she gazed into my eyes. "I can see that because of that, you're even stronger than I thought possible. Because you didn't understand your power, you didn't rely on it. You figured out for yourself, what works for you," My grandmother, looked at the ornate silver watch on her wrist as it buzzed. She pushed her chair away from the table and stood, carefully placing the sleeping feline on the chair cushion as she did. "I'm sorry, I know you've more questions, and there's so much I want to tell you. Further discussion will have to wait as unfortunately we both have errands to run today. Your return to Misty Vale changes things, for the better. Come for tea at 5pm this evening, and I'll answer any questions you have," Her fingers brushed my arm, a spark of energy and understanding flowed through my body. As if a door unlocked, and information downloaded into my brain. A reel of pictures and places spun in front of my eyes, but instead of feeling dizzy, I felt a sense of balance I hadn't known was missing.

Sprinkles sat bolt upright. Esmerelda leapt off the chair and back into the closest bush, an oversized geranium with bright red flowers. I wanted to stay and listen to Hazel speak and never leave her side. Reluctantly I joined her as she led me to the gate. "I'll be here. Do you want me to bring anything?"

"I've thirty-eight years of spoiling my granddaughter to make up for. Just bring yourself." Her eyes sparkled with love.

My feet hardly touched the ground, as Sprinkles and I retraced our steps to the cottage. My energy level, calmer than normal, my head no longer ached, even my audacious pup seemed quieter, happy to walk along snuffling the ground, without barking at everything that moved. There were still many questions, but I'd an unusual sense of belonging, and an understanding of aspects of my life which made no sense for such a long time. "Okay Sprinkles, home time for you, keep an eye out for visitors, I'll be back after lunch." My plans included finding Ned, having a coffee and a cupcake, visiting the library and the craft shop. All while letting the connection with Hazel sink in.

"That policeman called in again," Margot called from her little seat under the weeping willow tree. Leant over a little foot stool she used as a work bench, she had four little pots set up, half full of dirt, a bag of potting mix on one side. The dirt under her nails, and halfway up her elbows an indication of how long she'd been sitting there. A rack of plants behind her further evidence of her mornings work.

"Thanks Margot. What have you got planted up this time?" I asked conversationally.

"Geraniums, rosemary, and lavender. All woody cuttings at the time of the year." It was easy to picture her years ago, as a schoolteacher. She'd that way of speaking, it felt like she was sharing important knowledge, even in the everyday conversations. The way she peered over the top of her glasses sent a shiver down my spine.

Though I'd never settled in one place for long, I'd always felt drawn to plants. Most of the plants in my garden were similar to those in Hazel's, and Margot's. Were we family as well? I shook my head, that's crazy, lots of people love easy to grow flowers and herbs. I'm not related to everyone. "I love your plants. Can I buy some? When they're ready of course."

Margot gave me that look, over the top of her glasses. "Yes, you can buy some plants, though we both know you've as much of a green thumb as I."

Not knowing how to answer, I smiled. "I'm going for a walk, do you need groceries, or anything from the shops?"

"I'm good, but thanks for asking," Margot turned to her left, indicating the completion of our conversation.

I couldn't get the idea of Margot and I being related out of my head. Could she be my aunt? Misty Vale had more than one person or family with similar skillsets, and while there were likely people who were related to me, it didn't mean everyone with similar skills were. Hazel would fill me in, I needed to be patient. It's just that now I knew I belonged here, I was impatient to know everything there was to know, about where I fitted in. I squinted, as a flash of sunlight reflecting on a parked car shone in my eyes. I turned my head, blinking as the bright spots on my eyes dissipated. As I did, I noticed Marigold entering the empty shop on the corner. I turned to go and say hi, as Florence and the two women from the café, the blonde and the darker haired woman, dressed this time in matching red dresses followed Marigold into the building.

Chapter Nineteen

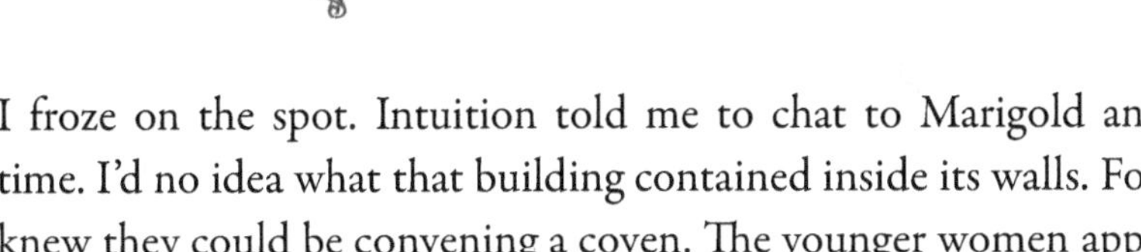

I froze on the spot. Intuition told me to chat to Marigold another time. I'd no idea what that building contained inside its walls. For all I knew they could be convening a coven. The younger women appeared as bossy and opinionated as Florence. On the other hand, it could be an innocent meeting. She and Marigold were members of so many local groups.

My instincts told me it wasn't a regular meeting that called those women into that building so early in the morning. I considered trying to eavesdrop, but there was nowhere to position myself out of sight at the front of the building. I didn't fancy being stuck at the back or the side without an escape plan. Curious, but certain it'd all soon fall into place, I resumed on my initial path, to the café.

"Jane, how did you go with those craft kits?" Cathy called from the front of *The Crafty Owl,* as she hung green sparkly tinsel across the front door. Little white sparkly star stickers glittered from under the tinsel.

"I've been caught up on other tasks, but I'm looking forward to starting them when I get a chance," I smiled. Three women in jeans, checked shirts and straw hats walked past me into the store. Cathy waved to me as she followed them in. My intuition told me they were farmers wives, earth elementals and avid crafters. I thought about the two younger women with Florence, trying to get a sense of who they were. Like a blank screen on a television, I got nothing but static.

I couldn't resist the idea of a cuppa and cake at *The Milky Bar*. I messaged Ned, as I walked through the door, asking if he was free to join me.

"Hi Jane," Jess greeted me as she hurried past with a tray of mini milkshakes. She handed them out to five children who sat crossed legged on large cushions in one corner of the café. The children were staring, their eyes wide in fascination, at a young woman dressed as a Christmas elf. Behind her stood a skinny silver Christmas tree decorated with red and purple baubles. Strings of little coloured lights hung around the ceiling of the café, and the new display case held a village of gingerbread houses.

"The café looks amazing Jess. When did you find the time to decorate?" I asked as she returned to the counter.

"I had helpers. The local year twelve cohort wanted to do something other than wrap the town in toilet paper and seeing as Christmas characters kept popping up around town, they offered to create Christmas in the café," she gestured to the elf, reading a large Christmas picture book to the children. "Cherie is one of the graduates from the childcare educator's vocational course. She offered to bring story time to the café." Jess picked up a pen, "What would you like today?"

"An iced coffee today I think, for something different. No cake, yet, though I might change my mind later. Can I pay for whatever Ned drinks, for next time he pops in. I owe him one from the other day."

"Sure thing," Jess scribbled my order on the paper near the register.

The bell above the door jangled and a line quickly formed behind me. I chose a table not too close to story time, but one where I could watch people coming and going. The spot in the middle of my forehead, I'd heard referred to as *the third eye*, started tingling. I raised my finger to it, but lowered it again, instinctively knowing not to rub my forehead. I counted twelve customers at the counter, and another seven already seated, the busiest I'd seen the café, though I tended to steer clear of peak times, generally.

After meeting Hazel I was keen to learn as much as I could about the town and the people in it. Not because I could be related to them, but I wanted to know more about how magic, my magic, worked. The fear I normally associated with being out in public wasn't there anymore.

I tuned into the auras of those around me, picking up snippets of conversation. Feeling, rather than seeing the light hues of colour, the auras gave a whole new dimension to the café as pale blues, greens, and purples shimmered around most of the customers. A few residents emitted orangey yellow glows, one red, and one radiated a dark shade of brown. I involuntarily shuddered and looked away, making a mental note to ask Hazel about what I could see. I'd a vague knowledge of auras, and knew the colours related to our feelings, emotions, and in some cases health. Could auras reveal more about a person, and their motivations?

The colours above the seated children bounced and shimmered like a rainbow. The hair on my arm tingled and I turned back to the door. Ned was in line, chatting with the two women dressed in red. The blonde lady kept tapping the policeman on the arm, giggling at his words. Her fake smile reminded me of the way Florence behaved when she coerced people to do as she asked. The brunette surveyed the other customers. I watched as her deep blue eyes moved from one person to another. Who was she looking for? I didn't like either woman, didn't trust them, after overhearing their conversation. Was I jealous they were talking to the handsome policeman? No, but I could no longer fool myself that I wasn't smitten with my new friend. Finally, the women arrived at the front of the line and placed their order, reluctantly leaving Ned to place his.

"You look much better today, Jane. Thanks for the cuppa, you didn't have to do that," The handsome policeman carried two takeaway mugs as he joined me at my table. "Jess had these ready and I offered to bring them over. You were right about those ladies; there's something off about them."

"I'm feeling so much better, thank you. I managed to solve part of the mystery. Did you manage to find out who they are or why they're in town?" I indicated the two women in red, seated near the children's story time.

"Mindy and Cindy are interested in setting up a business locally, something about event planning, which sounds too upmarket for Misty Vale, but I guess people are always looking for quirky and different themes for birthday parties, etc. According to them anyway," he leant forward, taking a sip of his coffee. "So, what did you figure out, mystery wise?"

Confiding in people wasn't what I did, ever, but Ned was a policeman, and my intuition told me he could be trusted. "Do you know Hazel Thorne?" I decided to start with a question.

"Everyone who's lived here awhile has heard of her. She's the real matriarch of Misty Vale. Something happened years ago that caused her to retreat and relinquish her role in the village. Florence took advantage of Hazel's family circumstances. When Hazel stepped down, Florence, her husband, and members of the founding families took over. Not ruling exactly but slowly moulding the committees into their vision of the village," Ned sipped his coffee, a faraway look in his eyes. "I always wondered why Hazel stepped down, she'd done so much for the village, then she just disappeared. Such a shame."

I heard the admiration in his voice. It made me a little proud. Of the grandmother I'd only met a few hours ago. A little sad that we'd only just met, and for the many wasted years. The irony that she'd devoted part of her life to helping other villagers, but she couldn't help her own family.

"Jane?" Ned broke through my thoughts, as I was questioning my parents' motives.

"Oh, yes, sorry. Hazel Thorne is my grandmother," I couldn't help but chuckle at the look of disbelief that crossed the policeman's face. "I met her for the first time today. At 23 North Street, which as it turns out is not the meeting place for a coven, after all. Hazel is my mysterious benefactor; she delivered the key, the photographs, and documents." I paused, savouring the caramel flavoured coffee. "There was a pact between my parents and grandmother that I wasn't to know about my heritage," I rolled my eyes, attempting to hide the hurt I felt at that knowledge.

"That's a lot," Ned's eyes frowned, as his brain processed the information. I sensed another emotion, care, concern for me, maybe. I wasn't used to reading my own emotions, or how other people were feeling.

"It is." I agreed, "That's the short version. I'll find out more tonight. I'm meeting her for dinner. Oh, and did I tell you? Margot suggested that maybe it's the Kennys, retired schoolteachers, who are breathing life into the Christmas characters."

Ned looked up from where he'd been staring at his cup. "The Kenny'? I should have checked to see if they were home," he scribbled a few words in his notepad. "So, the animated characters were coincidental and not distractions after all."

"Maybe. I'm not convinced. It's too convenient. I don't know the Kennys; would they go to all this trouble to create Christmas cheer?" I paused, drinking some of the icy cold coffee. "What updates do you have, that you can share with me, about what's going on in the village? Are there any suspects for the fire, and does the river still flow lemonade?" I would've asked more questions, but five elf like characters, no bigger than a metre tall, ran through the café. Thinner than the elves I thought I saw earlier, these weren't dressed in orange. They looked more like children than magical creatures. Without a sound they scooted over to the story time mat. Each elf chose a child and sat next to them.

Sophie entered just after the small creatures, beckoning for Ned to join her. "Sorry," he shrugged apologetically. As they conferred quietly in the corner, my eyes wandered around the café. It buzzed with the energy of pre-Christmas anticipation. Not just the excitable energy of the children, the adults in the shop appeared more animated and enthusiastic than usual.

I found it difficult to focus on the café, the mystery, and even my newfound family. All I could think about was Ned, his deep brown eyes, and how I wanted to run my fingers through his thick wavy hair. I felt the tension, even as he stood a couple of metres away. This budding attraction wasn't the only reason why I wanted to solve the mystery. I'd become fiercely protective of the residents, I wanted to find answers, to ensure the safety of the village.

Sophie smiled at me as she left the café. I found myself grinning as Ned returned to the table. "I'd be keen to know what else you find out, that relates to the mysterious goings on around the village. I still can't get my head around Hazel being your grandmother. You do realise that means you belong to one of the founding families. "My dad lived here his whole life, and I've been here most of mine. Except for a stint in the big smoke. I'm not from a founding family. Edwards don't have any specific skills, just a sense of auras, people's moods and motivations," he peered into the bottom of his mug, draining the last few drops of coffee. "Does that mean your skills are similar to Hazel's?" Before I could answer his mobile beeped.

Reading the message, the policeman stood, as did I, torn between staying and listening to conversations around me and wanting some quiet time in the peace of my cottage. "I'm not sure what her skills are. It turns out both my parents were from the founding families as they're called. I've a few skills I haven't worked out yet, but I get the impression that's all about to change."

Ned indicated the empty drinks. "Thanks for that. It's my turn next time. I'd love to stay and chat, but Sophie's been called to another drama. Fairy floss and lollipops growing on trees. The main problem is the number of children trying to climb the trees, some of them are quite high."

"That's quite a challenge," I smiled at the idea of Ned trying to stop a group of kids vying for sweets. "I'm heading to the library for more research, as tempting as it would be to go home and curl up with a good book."

Chapter Twenty

Ned and I exited the café at the same time. I drew in a quick breath, blinked, and rubbed my eyes, as Ned's mobile beeped again. "I don't think it's the Kenny's," the policeman said drily. In front of us, marching down the middle of the street in an impromptu and unadvertised street parade were toy nutcracker soldiers, glorious in black, white and gold uniforms; gingerbread men and women with large candied buttons, and colourful ribbons and bows; elves dressed in orange, green and red, with bells on their hats; snowmen, unmelted despite the heat; and a woman who looked like Mrs Claus. Her dress consisted of many layers of red, a white apron with real, not embroidered, candy canes, and reindeer, with bells on their harnesses.

People spilled out from the café behind us, and from the other shops on the street, as news of the spectacle spread around the village. People lined along the footpath, across the side streets, and even joining in on the parade. As I recovered from the initial shock, I noticed more characters. Carollers with hymn sheets, dressed in formal summer clothes rather than the traditional winter garb normally associated with Christmas singing. Two fairies, full people sized, not tiny, waving their wands, in sparkly pink summer dresses; a few other people, some dressed as witches, in black, with pointy hats and carrying broomsticks, with pumpkins rolling at their feet; and too many to count wooden and knitted toys, who all appeared to be sentient, waving and smiling as they passed by.

"What the?" I concurred with the sentiments of those around me, most of whom were snapping photos of the procession. Where on earth had these creatures come from, and where were they headed?

"I agree," Ned glanced at the screen of his mobile. "Sophie's found what looks like a giant gingerbread house, on the vacant block in Glebe Street. She can't get inside, it's cordoned off with large Christmas candy canes, more than a metre tall, Christmas lights, tinsel, and more soldier sentries. Residents living on that street have confirmed it's where this group originated from. Sophie's staying there to monitor the situation from that end."

I surveyed our surroundings. Although the crowd on the path were three deep, people were behaving nicely, no pushing or shoving; they appeared mesmerised by the event. "We could squeeze past everyone and follow the parade. I will, if you want to stay here and make sure there's no ruckus." People were still arriving, and the procession of characters showed no signs of ending.

"If you don't mind, that'd be helpful. I'll follow once the procession comes to an end. Just be careful. I know you have powers, but this is an awful lot of people, anything could happen. We don't know who's behind this, or their motivation," my friend sounded worn, exhausted.

With a wave that said I agreed and understood, I turned and moved along the path, weaving in and around villagers as they talked, pointed, and photographed the parade. Cars, parked on the side streets, their drivers and passengers left with no choice but to stop and watch the goings on. Rather than looking miffed at the change to their schedule, they appeared to be caught up in the contagious excitement of the procession. I took a closer look at the people around me. No one looked grumpy or put out. Everyone was beaming, like small children on Christmas morning.

Somewhere in my brain a lightbulb went on. Could this be the work of those two women who wanted the town to be known for craft and Christmas? Did they orchestrate the parade to encourage the atmosphere? Were they working alone, or with others? Possibly Florence and her cronies. Were there others? This undertaking wasn't some small thing.

It didn't take long for me to find the parade's destination. A few hundred yards from the café stood a Santa grotto. For a moment I couldn't place what normally stood on the site.

"How clever," a woman in her mid-twenties said to the two school aged children whose hands she was holding onto. The children, a boy and a girl aged around ten if I guessed correctly, leaned in to listen. "Those buildings are the old infant school classrooms, the school your dad and I went to, before all the classes moved to where you go to school. Someone has decorated them to look like Santa's home."

A woman a little younger than me, just in front of where I stood, whispered to her friend, "How did they attach the tinsel, lights and candy canes? It looks like they've created an electric fence – clever – people will stop and think before following the parade."

I realised she was correct about the transformation of the old school buildings, and the fence designed to keep us out, or the characters in. Watching the creatures as they entered the site, I admired the craftsmanship. The creator paid an incredible amount of attention to detail. As the participants from the parade passed through the open gate, they disappeared into one of the many buildings. It became impossible to see any trace of the snowmen, carollers, reindeer or other creatures that had been on public display seconds before. Nutcracker soldiers peeled off and instead of entering a building they stood at intervals along the electric light fence line. Rather than looking ominous, they appeared calm, like the guards at Buckingham Palace. I took a quick photo and sent a text to Ned, so he knew what was happening at this end.

In under ten minutes, the toy soldiers were the only evidence of the parade. The grotto in front of me lit up with all the decorations I'd expect to see in a Christmas village. People milled around, unsure whether to go back to their lives, or to wait and see what happened next.

"We need to go," An older man told his young charge. "Your mother will be wondering where we are. How about we ask her if we can come back later?"

The young boy nodded solemnly, "Okay Grandpa."

One question I couldn't shake – why? If the parade was designed as a publicity stunt to bring tourists into town, shouldn't someone be out in front spruiking about our amazingly magical village? As if on cue, the door to the main building in the grotto opened and Florence, dressed in red as Mrs Claus, and Mindy and Cindy, still in their red dresses, emerged. The blonde woman held a sophisticated digital camera.

The three women positioned themselves on the wooden verandah, so Florence faced the crowd, being filmed by blondie. The other woman held her mobile phone, capturing Florence from another angle. "It's great to see so many villagers out celebrating the festive spirit, and the unique creative atmosphere that is woven throughout this amazing place we are blessed to call home. Our village has been through a lot, and I know you agree with me that we lost our way for a while. I'm pleased to announce that now, with the support of my wonderfully talented daughters Cindy and Mindy, our village will receive the publicity it deserves. Visitors will flock to see the magic in our everyday, bringing a much-needed boost to our economy. More importantly, we will be able to bring the magic of the Misty Vale spirit to everyone." As her voice projected over those gathered, her fake smile fixed to her face, I mentally kicked myself for not noticing the family resemblance before.

Half the crowd gave a ruckus round of applause to their matriarch, while others murmured their dissent, "We don't want to have strangers traipsing around our town...our village is great the way it is...someone should have asked first...it's little more than smoke and mirrors...we need Hazel, she'll put Florence back in her place..." My heart flipped as

I realised, they were talking about my family, which considering I'd only just met her, I felt surprisingly protective of.

"Where is Hazel? Someone should fetch her." I turned to see who spoke, but I didn't recognise the gentleman, similar age to myself, dressed in dark jeans and a loud Christmas shirt.

"She's not been the same since her family ran out on her, leave her be. Florence is doing a good job," a woman I recognised from the craft workshops spoke up. Her dress was a patchwork of craft materials and tinsel.

"May I say something?" I recognised the voice and swung back to face the grotto. My grandmother, dressed in a dark green medieval style dress that sat just high enough above her feet to prevent her tripping on the fabric in her black lace boots, approached Florence. The younger women stepped back; their recording devices aimed at Hazel. A hush fell over the crowd as everyone waited to see what would happen next.

Chapter Twenty-One

Florence's face matched the colour of her dress, as her mouth opened, then closed again. A few seconds later her lips parted as she managed to get out one word, "Hazel."

My grandmother nodded curtly at the woman she'd managed to silence. "Thank you, Florence, and I appreciate you holding the fort while I couldn't maintain my role," Hazel turned, and facing the crowd, she made eye contact with the onlookers. As her eyes found mine, I nodded, recognising her question and giving her my unwavering and unlimited support. Anything to knock Florence off their pedestal. "I'm sure you'll be pleased to know that I'm ready to once again take on the role intended by virtue of my bloodline. Even more exciting than that, is the news that my granddaughter has returned home. We'll formally welcome her in a day or so, once we've had a chance to discuss things in more detail," she smiled at the audience. I felt the collective wave of relief that washed over the people standing around me. I heard a few harrumphs, and a few murmurings of displeasure, but most of the crowd welcomed Hazels words. Her back straight, with the poise of a leader, she returned to face Florence, "We need to have a chat. For now, the grotto can stay as it is, no more change for the village until the inhabitants can have a say on any initiatives. I trust you won't be sharing any of your recordings on social media sites, or any other media." That was an order, not a question, and not veiled in any way. My admiration for my ancestor grew tenfold.

Florence spoke, and while I couldn't hear her whispered words, the venom in them was evident from where I stood. I watched my grandmother raise her right hand in a gesture to stop. Once Florence's mouth closed, her lips pursed together so tightly her skin puckered, Hazel pointed, indicating the open gate. After a few seconds where I thought Florence might explode, her face redder than I thought possible for a human, she led her daughters down the steps, through the gate, and along the footpath back into town. Hazel stepped through the door, into the building and closed the door behind her.

Shifting my weight from foot to foot, to get the blood circulating around my body, I sensed the mood of the crowd. I allowed my third eye to open, not something I normally focused on, especially in a crowd. I noted the auras around most people were shades of green or purple. My sense was that a lot of those in the crowd were content with Hazel's return. Less than a third of the residents' auras were a murky orange to brown, depending on the depth of their disquiet with the change in dynamic. I focused on the mood of the crowd. I didn't need to hear their words to pick that most favoured Hazel to Florence, but that the Florence supporters were more likely to cause trouble.

Ever so slowly, people began to move away, back to whatever they were doing before the unplanned Christmas pageant. I followed the group heading back toward the shops in the main street, wishing for a mocha, but deciding against as I eyed the line up outside *The Milky Bar*. With shop doors wide open, as shop owners and customers stood talking about the last hours activity. "Do you think Hazel was telling the truth?" Asked a young man on the steps of the library. "Is her granddaughter back, and what does that mean for Misty Vale? I don't particularly like Florence, but at least she stepped up and did something."

"We don't want everyone flocking to town to see the results of magic," shuddered Kelly. "I'm willing to hear Hazel out. We don't know what happened all those years ago, and I personally don't like Florence's ulterior motives."

"Yes, well, I'm not too keen on hundreds of people flocking to the village either," the man said grumpily. "The village just needs someone to take control of all that stuff." He turned and headed into the library. Kelly saw me and waved, before turning to follow him.

I followed in step behind a group of women, I recognised from visits to *The Crafty Owl.* All wore jeans and red Christmas shirts, with tinsel tied around their raffia hats. "You could have knocked me over with a feather," said the lady on the left.

"You're not wrong! I wonder if Alexander and Sandra have returned to town as well?" said another.

"I heard they passed away a few years ago," said a third. "Which is such a shame. They were scared to bring their child up here, because of the family burden, er commitment."

The first woman who spoke, sounded a little upset, as she replied, "My family can be overwhelming. I understand it's a decision they didn't take lightly. Being pregnant and facing the wrath of the founding families, their own flesh and blood, I'm not sure I wouldn't have run away, given that set of circumstances."

"I heard that after they left town, other members of the founding families chose to change their last names," the smallest lady in the group spoke quietly. I had to move a little closer, to make sure I heard her properly.

"True," one of the women spoke a little louder. "I know Florence keeps records and tracks who's changed their names, left town, or moved into town. I'd hate to be new to town, and trying to figure out who's related to who."

Did Hazel keep similar records? I was tempted to speak up but decided instead to bide my time. I would defend my family, if needed, once I knew more about what place I held in the village. I tended to jump in feet first, which resulted in all sorts of trouble in the past. Then I ran on adrenaline and anxiety. Now, the energy flowing through me felt different. I'd found home, living close to the roots of my magic.

"Did you hear the news?" A group of three elves, dressed in red and green striped shirts and dark green trousers walked up beside me.

The taller of the three, whose hat reached the same height as my hip, added, "Hazel's granddaughter returned. They'll give Florence and her cronies a run for their money. I hope they run those two bossy, well-dressed young ladies out of town."

Up ahead a bell jangled loudly, and the elves raced off in the direction of the noise.

I reached the small alcove in the middle of the main street where a picnic table and park bench allowed a space to sit and rest a while. Popular with the older residents who needed a break during their shopping expedition. I sat on one corner of the bench seat. A couple of older men were crouched over a chess board that sat on the wooden table between them. I refrained from asking who was winning. Chess players tended to take their challenges seriously. "Do you mind if I sit here for a few minutes?" I asked, hoping I wasn't disturbing them.

"As long as you don't start waffling on about which woman should be in charge," the man in the short sleeved brown checkered shirt replied.

"Women in charge," chuckled the other man, in a blue polo shirt, as he moved one of his white chess pawns towards the black castle.

It made sense that people would be divided about Hazel and Florence. Both were strong personalities. The villagers would have been miffed, when Hazel stepped down all those years ago. If her birth right, my birth right, included a leadership position, what part did members of other families play? I counted on Hazel filling in the blanks when we met later.

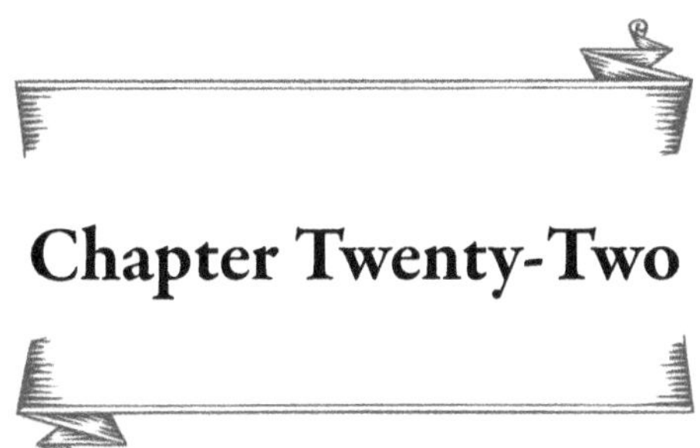

Chapter Twenty-Two

I realised I'd lost all track of time as I continued my walk home. My skin became hot and clammy as the heat of the sun told me it must be near the middle of the day. No wonder my stomach gurgled, asking for me to feed it. Once I left the main street behind, I could believe it was just another ordinary day in the village. Except for the random gingerbread person and snowman I passed on my way home.

I smiled as Mr Quin travelled long the footpath towards me on his motorised scooter. "Are you off to play chess today?"

"Yes, and to check out the goings on in town. Apparently, Hazel's granddaughter has returned to the village. Not that you'd know who I'm talking about, you're not from around these parts. The best bit is that Hazel tore strips off that Florence. Nasty woman, though the argument is she has done a lot for the village. Don't you worry though, Florence Hartly and her family have benefited from her actions." Mr Quin took one hand off the handlebars and shook a frail finger at me, "You didn't happen to see the street parade by any chance?"

"There were so many creatures, not just Christmas characters, but wooden toys, and knitted toys as well," An image of the unusual procession flashed in front of me, the vision still fresh in my mind.

"Couldn't have just been the work of the Kenny's," he mused. "I suppose someone could've used their magic to enchant that many items. Probably more than one person involved."

"Could Florence and her two daughters have achieved it?" I asked. "I know her daughters were keen to make the village a tourist destination."

Mr Quin frowned, "Now why in tarnation would they want to do that? Our village is just fine as it is, thank you very much." His worn straw hat bobbled on his skinny head. I resisted putting my hand out to stop it falling off, lest my movement startle the old man. "If that's the case I'm indebted to Hazel's granddaughter return. Hazel will make sure our village stays under the radar. We don't want reporters and tourists traipsing around, ruining everything."

Even if I wasn't related to the village matriarch, as just plain old Jane, I agreed with my neighbour. A couple of busloads every now and then, to admire our town's crafters was preferable to becoming a spectacle on local or national news and social media. "You enjoy your chess game Mr Quin. Most of the parade characters are in a makeshift grotto at the old school, so you shouldn't run into too much traffic." While Mr Quin looked frail, I'd seen him in his garden, and I had no doubt he could stand up for himself against cheeky elves or noisy carollers.

Clara Thorne

I spoke the name softly to myself as I walked the short distance back to my cottage. My name. It resonated with my soul more than *Jane Fairweather*, a name which had suffered the butt of jokes my entire school life. It didn't help that it appeared I conjured up stormy weather when I was cranky. Freak weather patterns happened whenever I felt particularly out of sorts. I could never be certain whether I'd caused them or if my moods mirrored my surroundings.

Did families generally have the same gifts? One of the many questions I had for Hazel. Who in town were members of the founding families? And what were their specific skillsets? Would those residents support Hazel or where they in Florence's corner?

As I unlocked my front door I exhaled, unaware I'd been holding my breath. Home, safe and without incident, and as far as I could ascertain, with no hidden packages or letters. "Hi Sprinkles," I patted my pup's head as he jumped at my legs. Cinnamon followed a few steps behind as we headed to the kitchen. Bert cheeped his greeting. "You guys are awesome. Such a wonderful welcome home," I popped some treats in their metal food bowls, hanging and new seed bell in Bert's cage. While they munched contentedly on their treats, I made myself a multigrain cheese and tomato sandwich. I rescued half a punnet of strawberries nearly at their best before date and whipped up a berry smoothie, adding honey, almond milk and a few mint leaves. I'd been neglecting my diet lately, what with all the cakes at the café. "Smoothies are the best," I told Sprinkles, waiting hopefully at my feet for any scraps. "Not just now, you just had your treat." Understanding words as much as Cinnamon did, Sprinkles decided instead to pounce on his ball. It escaped his paws and flew across the kitchen floor. He raced off after it, chasing it down towards the front door.

"Time for me to sit, eat and maybe read something," I told Bert. He chirped a response which I took to mean – *thank you for keeping me company*. On the kitchen table sat a pile of craft magazines I'd borrowed from the library. I flipped through the *Bumper Christmas Knitting Omnibus* as I ate my sandwich.

An hour later I'd marked the patterns I wanted to copy with post-it-notes. I counted fifteen in all, across the five magazines, which wasn't too bad. I knew where they were and could always borrow them again if the inspiration took me. The three craft kits I'd purchased earlier in the week sat at the end of the table. I'd splurged on a long pine table for the kitchen, and had often used it as a work bench for cutting material or putting craft projects together. "Resin, lip balm, candles," I read the directions and decided they'd all take too much brain power, now, with everything else that was going on. I settled for opening the kits, lining up the ingredients and instructions, in preparation for when I had more time.

My cuckoo clock chimed 3pm, with all the grace of a crazed wood-pecker. I dropped the glass jar that would one day hold a candle. It clunked on the table, thankfully without breaking. Sprinkles stuck his head up, to see what was going on. Cinnamon opened one eye. After quickly washing up my lunch dishes, I opted for a summery red shift dress with white flowers on it. Long, but not so long that I'd trip when walking to Hazel's house, I slipped sandals on my feet, and brushed my hair out, tucking it back into a messy bun.

All three of my furry and feathered babies were quiet, so I grabbed my keys, wallet and mobile and tiptoed outside, quietly closing the door behind me.

Chapter Twenty-Three

The air hung heavy as I left my house, as if a bush fire loomed on the horizon. An atmosphere of anticipation, an impending battle, which could change life forever in the village. The light grey clouds dotted around the sky contained a greeny hue I'd not previously noticed. A weird purple haze hung as if fog had settled over the village. "It's late afternoon in November," I whispered to myself, "There shouldn't be fog." A prickling sensation ran the length of my spine.

I turned to face the direction of my grandmother's house, my hands empty. I should have a gift to share. I meant to make more lemon slice but ran out of time. I leant over my low picket fence, and picked a bunch of geranium, rosemary, and lavender. *That's better.*

I heard a car pull up as I rounded the corner into North Street. "Do you need a lift somewhere?" Florence's voice unmistakable, she sat in the passenger seat of a black land rover. Her daughter with the blonde hair, Cindy, was the driver. I couldn't see properly through the dark tinted windows, but intuitively I knew Mindy sat in the back.

I took a step back. "Thank you for the offer, but no thank you," I didn't add that I'd nearly arrived at my destination. Was this a coincidence or had I been followed? I stood and waited for them to drive away before I continued walking. They appeared to be waiting for me, the car idled in the same spot, with no sign of moving. I wasn't sure if Hazel, or I, were ready for anyone, let alone Florence to know about our connection.

Sighing, I slowed my pace, clutching my posy, hoping they'd drive by. I could see my destination less than ten metres away. A movement caught my eye. Hazel walked, no marched, out from behind her gate and crossed the road to where I stood. I expected her to speak to Florence, instead she embraced me in a wonderfully warm welcoming hug. I ignored the burning on my cheeks, and the noise as Cindy floored the accelerator and sped away.

"They're horrible gossips, and what they don't know, they'll make up. I hope you don't mind. All their friends will know you're my granddaughter by the end of the day," my grandmother held me gently at arm's length. "I want to look at you, properly this time," she spoke softly looking me up and down. I knew she must be at least eighty years old, but she didn't look that much older than me. "Yes, I am that old," she took my arm and led me back across the road. "I'm eighty-eight next birthday as it happens. Luckily for me, my magic keeps me looking and feeling much younger than that," she closed the gate firmly behind us. I sensed the protection spell, woven throughout her property. She nodded, with a wink, "to keep out unwanted company."

"I keep wanting to pinch myself, that I found you, or you found me. I can't quite believe it, that I have family...and I have so many questions," I stammered, running out of words under my grandmother's gaze.

Hazel placed her hand on my arm, gently steering me onto the verandah. "I'll answer all your questions, but first, would you like some tea and scones?"

"That sounds lovely." My cheeks burned as I handed her my herbal bouquet, "I meant to make some lemon slice to bring over. This is all I have to share."

"Clara, I hope it's alright if I call you Clara, the herbs are perfect. Plants were a passion of your mothers. I could never manage to get mine to grow."

My heart swelled at my grandmother's praise. "What about all these? They're beautiful," I waved my hand at the plants that graced the verandah.

My grandmother smiled, "The plants I can grow are the easy ones, anything that requires more fuss and bother, I leave to others."

I sat in the same chair as earlier, while Hazel poured a light brown liquid from the teapot into the cup in front of me, "This tea is for understanding, intuition and higher knowledge." I couldn't place the aroma. Chamomile maybe, or lavender. My grandmother handed me a plate that held six scones. "These are just because they are yummy, no magical correspondences," she grinned. I chose one of the scones. On the plate in front of me, Hazel had placed a couple of dollops of cream and raspberry jam. The cake was warm and pulled apart easily. "There's plenty more of everything, so please eat, and drink, and I'll try to answer all your questions."

I concentrated on putting some raspberry and cream on the warm scone halves in front of me while my grandmother spoke, "I take it you've heard the term founding families?" I nodded, as my grandmother added jam and cream to her scone. "They were instrumental in making Misty Vale a haven for people with magical abilities. Farmers who possessed elemental magic. For generations they made a living off the land, successful in part because of their magic. Their gifts grew with each generation," she paused as she sipped her tea. I followed suit, the liquid immediately settling my soul. "The Deans, or Sparks, as they are known now, control fire. The Elliots, who manipulate air and wind, are known as Gale. Water elementals go by the name of Wilson and haven't changed their names much, except when they marry as was the case with Constance. Florence was a Murphy, an earth elemental. She married a Hartly, a family with questionable magic skills. Your genealogy, Devlins and Thornes, have spirit-based magic, which is rarer than the others." Hazel stopped; her eyes downcast. I didn't want to interrupt her thoughts. I sipped my tea.

After a few more moments silence, I asked, "My parents weren't meant to wed? Is it a rule that elementals can't marry each other?"

"At the time, it was considered taboo. For reasons we didn't fully understand, we, the leaders of the clans, continued to uphold the assumptions and decisions of our elders. Your parents' actions bought about more change than my stepping down. The council changed the rules with regards relationships between the families. By then it was too late. I tried to contact my son, your father, but neither he nor your mother would listen to me. They distrusted that Misty Vale would be a safe place for you to grow up. They felt strongly about you needing a 'normal' childhood. They made me reaffirm my vow not to contact you. I'd promised it and spent the next forty years regretting that vow. I always hoped that one day they'd decide to make contact, or return, if only for a visit." Another pause, my heart strings pulled tight at her pain. "They didn't."

My own heart tore a little, at the pain our family had experienced. My parents must have been just as heartbroken as Hazel. They hid all that from me. No wonder they both focused all their time and energy into their jobs. I wasn't sure what emotions to feel. I shuddered involuntarily, "My parents fell in love, become pregnant, left their hometown, changed their names, married, and didn't contact you, or any of their families and friends ever again. Such strong, decisive actions. It wasn't just that they weren't meant to marry, there must have been more behind it." I thought about the people I grew up with. "Mum and Dad were always at work or helping in the community. Even after working in the same places for over twenty years, they never took on leadership roles. Could part of the reason they stayed away be they didn't want the responsibility of being leaders? Dad would've inherited the role after you. Maybe they worried about me ending up with that same obligation and responsibility." The tingling in my fingers told me I was right.

"Yes, that thinking was a huge part of what motivated them. The elders back then, underestimated the feelings of the younger generation. In the wake of your parents' actions, others changed their surnames, or left town, searching for a freedom to live a life of their own choosing. Many ended up returning to the village. Ironically if your parents had stayed in contact with any of their peers, they would have understood about the changes and known it was safe to return."

With the burden of the past laid bare in front of us, we ate the remainder of our scones in amiable silence. Hazel passed me the plate, "Help yourself, if you feel like a second one."

"I will, and thank you, these are delicious I haven't had scones for years, Why and how did Florence end up stepping in?" I picked up a second, still warm, scone. The act of layering the simple home-made cake with jam and cream, an act of intention and concentration, as I focused on my grandmother's words.

She bowed her head, "I take full responsibility for that. I grieved for too long, and she took advantage of my absence. She saw an opportunity. Maybe in the beginning her plans were innocent, but over the years she took advantage of her leadership role in the village. With the encouragement of her husband, she accepted gifts and looked out for every possible opportunity for financial gain," Hazel pulled apart her second scone, slowly layering the jam and cream on one half, then the other. "Even in Misty Vale, people are happy for others to take the lead. They'll put up with a lot if it means they don't have to step into a leadership role."

"Then you can't take full responsibility," I responded slowly. "You say that no one stepped up to challenge Florence, so it sounds like it's everyone's fault, for allowing Florence to become so powerful, indispensable..." Pieces of the puzzle were slowly falling into place. "You said Florence was a Murphy, before she married?"

"Yes, a Murphy before she married a Hartly, one of the most unscrupulous families in the village. Norman and his brothers were always looking for ways to make money by exploiting the talents of our residents," Hazel paused, as she finished the last of her scone. She sipped her tea, gently placing the cup back in its saucer. I sensed she was searching for the right words. "Norman was killed when the girls, Cindy and Mindy, were teenagers. An accident at work, though Florence and the family were convinced that magic was the cause. He owned a real estate firm and several businesses, preying on those who couldn't make their repayments. A wall at a construction site fell on him. No one else was injured but he was crushed to death. The death was deemed an accident, and no one was charged. His brothers moved away and are business moguls in one of the big cities. Still using their magic to make millions. It's easier in a city to hide magic, and to get away with using it for less than noble intentions. The girls went away to boarding school and when they graduated, both started working in the city, with their uncles."

"I don't think I could've stayed, if I was Florence, the knowledge that someone in the village killed my husband, especially if my children moved away. You've just given me the answer to one of the mysteries I've been trying to puzzle out. I heard the girls talking about making Misty Vale a popular tourist destination for city folk," I clenched and unclenched my hands, an old habit to calm the energy that pounded through my body with no escaping it.

Chapter Twenty-Four

Hazel pushed her chair away from the table. "Come on, let's go for a walk, I want to hear about you." I followed her down the steps, taking the hand she held out for me. As we walked through the gate at the side of the house into her back garden. I gasped, not expecting the sight in front of me. "Do you like it?" she smiled, "I...we...own the whole block and while we don't call it a coven anymore, this is where we celebrate occasions like the equinox, the full moon, and other special dates."

We stood at the edge of large space in which eucalypts, conifers, and other grand trees, circled a clearing. Inside the circle, bushes and shrubs provided cozy outside spaces. Wooden benches positioned throughout the space, provided places to sit and read, chat, or think. A fire pit sat in the largest open area, with large stone seats planted at intervals around it. I clenched and unclenched my fists a few times, as a sense of home, of belonging, spread through my body. "Do you like it?" she asked, watching my fists with a wry smile on her face.

"It's like nothing I've ever seen, not in real life, though I've read about places like this, and seen movies," my words were having trouble forming proper sentences, as my emotions caught up with me. "The space is what, four or five normal sized backyards?"

My grandmother nodded.

"You've solved another mystery for me. You've used your garden as a meeting place, and Marigold gave me this address when I asked about covens in Misty Vale. Do you think she figured out who I was?" The pieces of the puzzle slowly clicked into place, as my brain caught up with what I saw, heard, and felt.

"I think she wanted someone to help her manage Florence," Hazel led me further into the clearing. "So, tell me about you," she nodded at my fists, still clenched shut. "Did you figure that out yourself or did someone show you?"

I looked at my hands as if for the first time, slowing uncurling them, putting them back at my sides. I shrugged, "It's just something I do when I feel...too much. It started when I was little. Other children teased me when things kept happening around me, breaking toys, vases falling over, other items would break, accidentally. The television, the radio, and other electrical things would randomly stop working. I'd feel...too much...and clenching my fists seemed to help."

Hazel took my hand and held it in her own for a few seconds. "Did your parents teach you anything, about our heritage, our skills or how to manage this type of thing?"

"No. I thought there was something terribly wrong with me, for years. So many things would happen around me, the weather would change, freak storms would cause damage. Children called me weird. My fiancé called off our wedding, and with no emotional support from my parents, no advice other than to work hard, focus on the practical, I left. As soon as I turned seventeen, I ran as far away as I could. Around the time of my thirtieth birthday, I figured out that magic of a kind did exist, and I had some of it. I still focused on the practical and worked hard at my job, solving crimes. When I had enough of work and saved enough money to travel again, I decided to see more of our country, I'd already travelled the world. I came upon this little village and felt drawn to stay. Now I understand why."

Silence. My connection with this woman I'd just met told me she was devastated, knowing how I'd suffered, because I'd not been taught how to deal with my abilities. I squeezed her hand. "You need to know that I don't blame you. I don't blame my parents either. I didn't understand why, but I knew they were running from something they couldn't talk about. Work was their focus, always. They did the best they could. I learnt from them, running away, and focusing on work. It wasn't a terrible existence," I turned in a circle, taking in the whole garden. "Did you create this yourself? It's amazing."

"Your great grandfather, my father, started it, and yes, I've added to it over the years. All the founding families have a similar garden where they gather, celebrate, and honour our ancestors. I've some books with maps and more information if you're interested." She brushed her hand over the biggest lavender bush I'd ever seen, releasing the soothing floral fragrance, "Is there anything specific about your magic that you want to ask?"

I thought about the question, "Yes, but not just now. I've worked out the basics myself. At the moment, it's enough that we've found each other. You've explained so much already. Tomorrow, maybe or the day after, I'll probably be asking questions."

"Would you like to come inside?" The back of Hazel's house appeared as non-descript as the front. With tall plants growing around the building, it felt safe, protected. A couple of stairs led into a glass walled verandah. Up close, the house seemed at least twice as big as my little cottage.

Did I want to enter my grandmother's house? "That'd be nice," I commented, following Hazel up the stairs. I thought of one question I'd been pondering for a while. "Was my dad an only child? From the photos you left for me, it looked like my mother had siblings, but my dad didn't."

Before she could answer, the sound of a mobile interrupted us. Hazel looked at the number on the screen. "Sorry, do you mind if I answer this?"

"Go ahead."

"Hello. Yes. We'll be right there," she closed the cover on her phone. "There's a problem, another fire. Will you come with me? Only if you're comfortable becoming known as my granddaughter. I promise, I'll answer your questions, as many as you have, as soon as I can."

"Of course I'll come. I'm surprisingly comfortable with this whole situation. Maybe because I dislike Florence so much, or because I've finally found where I belong." Impulsively, I hugged my grandmother, "There'll be plenty of time to talk about family, to read maps and books, after we sort out whatever is going on in town."

My grandmother grinned, "We're alike you and me. I promise to fill you in on as much family details as I can on our next visit. For example, your mother was a brilliant artist. She painted watercolours and exhibited them in local galleries. Your father loved to go bushwalking and created amazing sculptures out of wood. I have photographs."

"I'd love to see those photographs..."

The tinny ringing of my mobile interrupted me. My heart skipped a beat, whether because of everything my grandmother had shared about our family, or because the caller ID told me a handsome policeman was calling, I couldn't be sure.

"Hello," I smiled into the phone, sensing my grandmother watching me.

"Jane, it's Ned. Sorry to interrupt tea with your grandmother but are you both able to come down to the shops in Spirit Road? I'd appreciate it if you could."

Chapter Twenty-Five

As I climbed into the Kermit green coloured jeep that Hazel backed out of her wood framed garage, my heart pounded. My pulse raced as we headed to the scene of a fire, and I had no details of the extent of any damage. Soon everyone in town would know me as Hazel's granddaughter. In such a short time, I'd come to fiercely love, and felt such pride for this octogenarian. A strong willingness to stand beside her and to help the town, sat better with me than I expected.

"You're not the only one who'd prefer to be a hermit, stay inside with a furry menagerie. It's what I've been doing for far too long." I smiled as my grandmother read my thoughts. "No points in regrets, things happen for a reason. You're here now and we can do this together."

"Do you have any details of the fire?"

"All I know is it started in a vacant shop on the corner," Hazel swung her car into a spot in the car park behind *The Crafty Owl*. Quite a few people milled around their cars, hands shielding their faces from the late afternoon sun, staring at the dark grey smoke spewing from the shop on the corner.

Aware my fists were clenched; I drew a deep breath in and exhaled, "That's the building I saw Florence and Marigold entering the other day, with Cindy and Mindy. I tried to listen in, or see what they were doing, but I didn't want to get too close." My brain slowly sifted through the pieces of knowledge I'd collected over the last couple of days. "I heard the conversation between the younger women. They were hoping to get the families to sell something of value and then create a tourist spectacle of the village. Could they have started the fire, to get rid of evidence in the building?"

"Probably. Our families have several ancestral heirlooms that Florence could try to buy, in a bid to strengthen her role as matriarch. I'd be surprised if anyone would sell to her though. Our land and artifacts are sacred," Hazel opened her door, then turned back to me, "Are you ready?"

"Yep, let's do this," I jumped out of the jeep, falling into step beside her.

We trailed behind a well-dressed couple. "It's just not good enough," the woman in a pink pants suit frowned at the man in a navy jacket. "We came all the way out here, expecting the story of the year, to be told that it's all off and to go back to the city," Her voice carried over the car park, her stage whisper turning heads around us. "We're not going back without a story. Get the camera Nicholas, the microphone too, all the recording equipment, and meet me at the front of the building that's on fire. We're getting a story one way or another." Nicholas murmured something I couldn't hear and scuttled off to a black van parked at the front of the next row of cars.

"Oh dear," I whispered to Hazel. "I don't mind everyone knowing about me, but are you ready for what might come out about our family, with a reporter hell bent on making a name for herself?" My only living relative, was twice my age, and while she didn't look frail, I'd no idea if she suffered any health issues.

"No need to worry about me dear," she tightened her grip on my arm. "You're not the only one who uses physical actions to manage emotions and energy. I'm not as fragile as I look. I've hidden for far too long and its time I set the record straight," she stopped and turned, so her face close to mine. "Do you trust me? That I only want the best for you? That I'd never do or say anything to hurt you?"

I nodded slowly. Although I'd only met her earlier in the day, I did trust this woman in front of me. "Yes," I said, surprised at the strength in my voice.

"Then come on, let's sort this out. If I say anything you aren't sure about, please ask me, later, when we're by ourselves."

My pulse sent sparks of energy around my body. "Okay," I held her gaze, both of us acknowledging the unspoken bond – family. Our feet stomped across the car park, the determination causing ripples on the ground. Did anyone else notice? We followed the reporter down the side alley, towards the front of the store, where a crowd gathered.

"Excuse me," Nicholas's voice breathless as he quietly pushed past where we stood.

"Woohoo Jane, over here!" Florences voice grated, like scratching chalk along a chalkboard and getting your fingernails caught. Still dressed in red, she stood near the giant Christmas tree. She wasn't alone. Her daughters, changed into blue jeans and white shirts, flanked her sides. Marigold, dressed in a rusty brown dress dotted with tiny golden stars stood to one side with Gwennie and Constance. They were dressed in jeans, green Christmas shirts and tinsel, as if they'd all just arrived from a Christmas luncheon. "I didn't know you knew Hazel...Ooh..." I watched the recognition in her eyes. She turned to her daughters and whispered a few words, motioning for Marigold and the others to join her. I didn't need to hear the words to know what she'd said.

The reporter in pink hurried over to Florence, almost dragging Nicholas along with her. After a couple of seconds of hurried conversation, the reporter grabbed the microphone from Nicholas, motioning for him to turn on the recording device. "My name is Barbara Moore and I'm here in Misty Vale. Strange things have been happening here, and I've been asked to assist the residents to get to the bottom of the problem. It's important to me and my viewers that we uncover and report on the truth," she stepped back until she stood alongside Florence. "I'm here with Florence Hartly and other concerned residents. Florence, why don't you tell us exactly what's been happening in this quaint little village."

Florence's grin reminded me of a child who'd been told she could eat all the ice cream she wanted. "Thank you, Barbara. I'm so pleased you're here so we can tell our story. Misty Vale residents are happy keeping to ourselves, we don't like fuss and bother, but with everything that's happening we welcome the chance to set the record straight," she paused, before pointing to where Hazel and I were standing. "Those two women have conjured up Christmas creatures and brought storybook characters to life, creating pandemonium in town, in a desperate bid to bring tourists into the village. A move not supported by most of our residents," her strong voice would have carried over the crowd, even without the microphone.

All eyes turned towards where my grandmother and I stood, arms linked. Tears threatened to run down my face. I blinked as they escaped, making little rivulets down my cheeks. I squeezed Hazel's hand, holding up my free hand towards the reporter. "Barbara, is it? May I please say something?" The woman in pink zipped across the gap that separated us, so quickly I imagined the dust flying under her high heeled shoes. She shoved the microphone in front of my face. The stony look Florence gave me didn't faze me, though the lump in my throat constricted my breathing. "Florence just lied to you. As far as I've been able to figure it, it's Florence and her colleagues who've been creating the havoc we've witnessed in town over the last few days. I overheard a conversation between her daughters; they were plotting ideas for bringing tourists to our village and how much money they'd make. Before Florence can spread any more lies, I want to make one thing clear," I heard the silence, as everyone waited for me to continue. "I am Hazel's granddaughter. A fact I only discovered earlier today," I lowered my voice a tad as I directed my next words to Barbara. "Before you publish any of this information, I suggest that you fact check everything,

I'd hate your career to be short lived because you were sued for liable and misrepresenting the truth."

Chapter Twenty-Six

Like a tennis match, the crowd turned to Florence, waiting for her to respond. Her face turned five different shades of red, pink, purple, and orange as her mouth opened and shut a couple of times. Barbara stood in no man's land, trying to hedge her bets, undecided whether she should stay near me or move over to Florence.

Hazel solved the problem for the reporter, "I have something to add." Barbara leaned in with the microphone. Florence's face continued to change colour. "My name is Hazel Thorne. By virtue of my family heritage, I should've been more active in our community. Unfortunately, I let a family matter come between me and my duty to the village. My son married a local woman, and they chose to leave town with their unborn baby. I shouldn't have let myself grieve for so long, but I did. I take fully responsibility for that. Not for Florence's actions. They are hers alone. There are others in the community who could have stepped in but chose not to. What's done is done, we can't change the past. Now, my granddaughter and I want to work with anyone in the village who is willing to help us, to ensure that it remains a safe place for all its residents." I squeezed her hand as a cheer from the crowd shattered the silence following her words.

"Are you really going to let her get away with that? Hazel decides now that she wants to help...I've been the one who's done the hard work, made sure of everyone's safety, that the village ran smoothly, not her." Cindy and Mindy each took one arm, trying to lead their mother away from Barbara's microphone. She wriggled her arms, elbowing them in the stomach, until they let go. The reporter shoved past the younger women, pointing the microphone towards Florence.

"Why don't we all go about our normal business and let the firemen ensure the safety of this building," Hazel spoke firmly, without the aid of the microphone. "I know we've some things to figure out, as a village, but that can be done tomorrow or the day after. Go home and have a nice dinner with family, relax and don't worry about anything."

I didn't count the number of people who'd gathered, but as far as I could tell, reading their auras, most of them agreed with Hazel's words. Parents steered their children back to their cars, others huddled in groups, chatting quietly as their made their way back along the street to their homes, places of work, wherever they'd been before this latest incident drew them out. Hazel and I stood in a comfortable silence, hands entwined. "It feels like most of the crowd were okay with what we said," I broke the silence.

"It seems so, but we shall see. As a rule, most people are satisfied with whoever is willing to lead. They'll grumble sometimes but leave others to the hard work," A few seconds later she added, "I don't mean to sound bitter, and I of all people...I stepped down for so long, I have no right to sound so officious." As Hazel stopped speaking I looked to see what had caught her attention. A few people were still in the area. Barbara and Florence were talking furiously, whilst Nicholas, Cindy, and Mindy clearly wanted to be elsewhere. Ned stood with two men dressed in full fire-fighting garb. He wrote in his notebook as they pointed at something in the soggy ruin of what used to be the shop on the corner. A group of six people, older than me, but younger than Hazel, were staring at us from their position a few metres away. "This will be interesting," whispered Hazel, as a couple of the group headed towards us. She held her head high, her hands crossed gently in front of her.

Before I could respond, a couple of residents, that I recognised only by sight, were standing in front of us. The woman, with shoulder length, light brown hair, tied in a neat ponytail, wore knee length khaki pants and a white linen shirt. The gentleman, whose hair was more grey than any other colour, wore jeans and a light blue shirt. I estimated their ages as closer to my parents, had they still been alive. A few metres away, the residents they'd been standing with watched the interaction.

"Hazel," the woman's words contained no warmth, her face no hint of a smile. The man tilted his head ever so slightly in recognition.

"Bernadette, Ross," Hazel responded in the same curt manner.

This could take forever, but I knew it wasn't my place to hurry things along. Bernadette turned to me, "We were in the same year at school as your parents. We're sorry to hear that they passed away. I always held out hope that they'd one day return to Misty Vale."

I wasn't sure of the correct response to that comment. "Thank you. I'm Jane...er...although I guess my name is really Clara. I'm still getting used to it," I stopped, unsure of how much information to share with two strangers. Hazel knew them, but I couldn't tell if she trusted them or merely tolerated them. The interaction was difficult to read.

Bernadette nodded curtly. The next question she addressed to Hazel. "Are you back for good or is this another half-hearted attempt?" Ross nudged the woman's arm before she could finish her question.

"I didn't see or hear that you decided to step up for the benefit of the town either Bernadette Murphy," Hazel retorted. "Neither did you Ross Dean," she added, a little less venom in her voice. "I don't need to justify myself to you or anyone else, any more than you need to justify your behaviour to me. I propose a truce until we fix up things around here." Her steely grey green eyes stared down Bernadette, who averted her eyes first.

"What exactly are you suggesting needs fixing, in your opinion?" The fingers on my left hand clenched and loosened. Phew, this Bernadette woman was hard work.

I took one step forward, a little closer to Bernadette, hoping she felt more discomfort than I did at my action. "May I make a suggestion?"

Ross leaned to his right, subtly touching Bernadette's arm. "Please do."

I indicated the group who were trying not to look obvious, as they stared our way. "Do those people belong to original Misty Vale families as well? Are they waiting for you to report back to them on what we say here?"

Bernadette's face reddened in anger; Ross bowed his head a little. "They are," he responded, casting a sideways glance at them.

"I've only lived here for a few months, and over the last week or so, we've seen break-ins, fires, the river turned to lemonade, and a parade of magical creatures. The last two events aren't too bad on the scale of things, but I'd like to see us work out exactly what's happening and who's behind it all. I assume your residents group want to too?" I sensed Hazel's approval. I hoped she'd be just as pleased with my proposal. "I suggest we call a meeting of the members of the founding families and talk about how we're going to resolve the issues. Can you organise a meeting room, somewhere big enough to fit whoever you think needs to be there?" I chose to address Ross and Bernadette equally, out of respect for their standing in the village, rather than ignore the woman for her rude behaviour. I hoped for an easy way to resolve the emotive situation.

Ross glanced at Bernadette. The woman's face still the colour of a ripe tomato, she opened her mouth and closed it again. I sensed she was considering her options. "Very well," she spoke sternly. "10am sharp tomorrow morning. The usual place," she nodded curtly to Hazel. "She can tell you where that is. We'll let the others know." Without waiting for a response, Bernadette nudged Ross with her elbow and headed back to the others.

"Hazel, Clara," Ross held out his hand, shaking Hazel's hand, then mine, before joining Bernadette.

Chapter Twenty-Seven

"Do you feel like a walk?" Hazel asked, linking her arm through mine. Now that my heart decided I didn't need to be on high alert, the loud thumping in my ears subsided, I took in my surroundings. My eyes focused on the building that had been the victim of a firebug. Behind Bernadette and Ross, Ned and the firemen were still huddled. One of the firemen held a hose, probably a precaution in case any of the embers reignited. The older officer, taller than Ned, with greying hair and a white beard, held a tablet in one hand, gesturing to what remained of the building with the other. He and Ned walked towards the charred remains of the front door, then down the side of the building towards the car park.

I was curious as to the cause of the fire, but that conversation could wait. My pulse did quicken a little at the thought of another opportunity to sit with Ned. I felt the heat rise in my cheeks as I imagined how nice it would be to hold his hand. I squeezed my eyes shut, opening them again quickly, clearing the image and focusing on my grandmother.

"That would be lovely, lead the way." With a new appreciation of how long Hazel had called this village home, I took in my surroundings with a more discerning point of view. "Have you always lived in Misty Vale?"

"Yes, although I travelled a little before your father came along. I often thought about leaving, after he and your mother left town, but I stayed in case they ever decided to return. When your grandfather passed away, I focused all my time and energy into the green space, in a way it made me feel closer to him, your father, and you." The sadness in her voice wrenched at my heart strings.

I heard my voice tremble as I asked, "Are my mother's family still in the area?" The lump in my throat was back.

"Your grandparents decided to move away, back to Scotland, a place they both loved when they travelled as young newlyweds. I didn't keep track of where her sister and brother moved to. Coincidentally, Margot, who lives next door, is a distant cousin of yours." A slight smile played on her face, "I'm so pleased you're here, and I'm sorry I can't reunite you with any other family members."

"That's okay. I've found you, or you found me, and that's more than I could have ever asked for." I wanted to ask if she regretted the decision to stay, and to keep the vow she made, not to contact me. My stomach wound itself in knots, preventing me from getting the words out. Instead, I asked, "Over the years, has the village changed much? Do many people move to the bigger towns, or come here from other places?"

"Yes, although we haven't experienced as much change as you'd have noticed in the bigger cities. Misty Vale residents appreciate the quaintness of village life. I've many regrets, but that I stayed, and we found each other, isn't one of them." As she spoke, I realised she'd again read my thoughts and answered my unasked question. "The changes in our village have been subtle. Farming practices have changed and way business occurs is assisted by new technologies. The same happens in every town, village and city. It's the creativity of the residents that make this town unique. Their ability to manipulate the elements. Most residents use their skills wisely, with consideration for the community. Every so often there are those who push the boundaries, creating fuss and dramas. As is the way of things, these challenges normally fizzle out back to nothing." Hazel pointed to the open door of the craft shop, "The craft shop is a good example of a new idea that is working well within our village. Cathy is a newcomer who fell in love with the village, noticed an opportunity, and her craft shop is a hit with our crafty residents. We were always a creative bunch, and now, with her store providing easy access to such a wide variety of craft supplies, our residents are winning prizes, locally and further afield."

"The Broom Factory is another example. From what I can tell, people travel to Misty Vale for good quality old fashioned millet brooms, and craft items," I recalled hearing customers talking in the café.

"Exactly the type of initiative I'm talking about," my grandmother agreed. "All our businesses benefit from the occasional increased foot traffic. Not too many visitors, and not a gaudy tourist attraction, as Florence's daughters would prefer to see our village turn into."

Cathy closed and locked the door of her shop behind her, smiling as she saw us. "Jane, Hazel, I didn't know you knew each other. It's lovely to see you both. It's been a quite an eventful day and now that the fire is no longer a threat, I'm heading home for a rest."

"It's nice to see you too Cathy." I could tell the smile on Hazel's face was genuine. "I'll be in later the week to pick up some more magazines and furniture." I was intrigued, there was still so much I didn't know about my grandmother. Or that Cathy's shop sold furniture.

Noticing my puzzled look, Cathy grinned, "You obviously haven't seen the magic Hazel creates with old bits and pieces, scraps that others would throw away. Miniatures," she prompted, as I clearly hadn't figured out what she was talking about.

I looked from one woman to the other. "I look forward to figuring out the code you are both speaking," I laughed.

While I normally limited my outings to *The Crafty Owl, The Milky Bar,* the library and occasional trip to the nursery, walking along the main street with my relative fascinated me. I saw the village through her eyes. She'd walked this path many times in her long lifetime. The shops along the street included a newsagent, a chemist, a hardware store, the post office, a couple of dress shops, one that sold footwear and hats, another specialising in electrical appliances and computers, a solicitor, a financial advisor, a seamstress, and a couple of pubs. As we walked, she pointed to the buildings and shared snippets of the town's history.

"Bruce at the hardware store, is another of our newer residents. He's a distant relative of the Dean family. He started off on the wrong foot, trying to set up a men's shed and getting the local's involved," she sighed. "Our residents don't like to be told what to do, especially by newcomers. To his credit, he learnt from his error, toned down his enthusiasm and listened to what his customers needed. Employing the local teens earned him more kudos in the community." The front of the hardware store was decorated with a Santa sleigh, reindeer, and fake snow. I loved the sign, which asked for donations of non-perishable food and toys for a local charity to hand out at Christmastime.

"See that dress shop, *Witchy Woo Fashions,* Glenda Murphy is a local artist, who started out painting watercolours, moved on to sculptures, and now she's forty something, she decided to start a clothes shop, with a point of difference," Hazel pointed to the mannequins in the window, one dressed in a patchwork robe, the other in a dress made from tinsel. "She works with the local high school and college fashion students. Using old, donated clothes as templates, they create wearable works of art. The end results are surprisingly popular."

I peered closely at the fabric on the store dummies. The delicate stitching evident, even through the thick window glass. "So many talented people," I murmured.

"We're not all as talented as I'm making it sound," Hazel admitted. "Most of us are as normal as the next person. Albeit with a smidge of magic."

A lightbulb switched on in my brain. "You make it sound like not everyone who possess magical abilities intuitively know how to use their magic. Are there others, like me, who weren't taught by their parents? How did they learn? Are magic lessons provided in the local schools?"

"It depends. Most parents would give their children basic lessons. The high school provides some opportunities for students to practice elemental magic, as an elective subject. There is a boarding school, in a nearby city, where some parents choose to send their children to learn the craft. Like a finishing school for witches. We've an informal community mentoring system here which works for many," Hazel paused as we neared *The Milky Bar*. "I know I promised you a dinner, and we only got to eat scones. Do you fancy whatever the special is this evening?"

"I didn't realise Jess stayed open late," My head spun, with all the information Hazel shared. I felt part of the community, part of a family. A very pleasant feeling. My stomach gurgled so loudly; I wondered if she heard it. "I'm suddenly starving, let's eat."

Quite a few other people had the same idea. The café looked larger than normal, there were more tables and seats than I was used to seeing. "It this an illusion?"

"Elvin magic," My grandmother confirmed. "Have you ever wondered how Jess manages to cook and serve, with only her mother to help? She's part elf, and her café is a place where bored elves can choose to work. No elf ever has to work for humans. They've their own community systems in place, providing enough wealth for them live comfortably. When they choose to help in local businesses, we rarely see them. Despite the bad publicity they attract, elves are quire shy, and friendly."

I touched my fingers to my temples, rubbing slightly to ease the pressure building up behind my eyes. "Long day, lots of information, and not enough water," I explained as Hazel eyed me with concern.

"Jane, Hazel, it's lovely to see you both. Tonight's special is pizza. We have meat lovers, or vegetarian. There's a small table near the back wall. If you want to eat in that is," Jess smiled.

I looked at Hazel. "How about vegetarian pizza and a jug of ginger beer?"

Hazel nodded.

"We'll eat here," I added, as I handed Jess the money for our meal.

"Is it just me, or does it feel like there are about ten pairs of eyes watching us?" I asked my grandmother as we arrived at our table.

"They're watching us. Most people know who I am, even though I tend to stay home as much as possible. We caused quite a stir earlier today. Try to pay no attention to them," Hazel sat facing the café, I joined her on the bench seat attached to the back wall. "I'm looking forward to the pizza."

"I'm used to being watched or at least thinking that I'm being watched. I learnt long ago that I can't influence how other people think or feel," I made light of it, though I was sure that my grandmother could see through my bravado to the emotions, raw, just beneath the surface.

Chapter Twenty-Eight

A totally different emotion bubbled to the surface a few minutes later as the doorbell jangled and Ned and Sophie walked through. As much as I loved meeting my dad's mother, I blushed, knowing she probably picked up on my feelings. We shared such a strong bond. Sophie lined up at the counter, while Ned approached us.

"Ned," my grandmother nodded to the policeman. "Please, sit with us. There's room for your colleague too," she pointed to the chair closest to me.

"Hazel, thank you, it's been a long afternoon, and I'd like to sit a while." He plopped himself on the offered seat, turned to me, and smiled, "I was hoping to catch up with you."

I wasn't sure how to respond to Ned, luckily, Jess arrived with our pizza, and I didn't have to. "Would you like another pizza? And more plates?" she asked Ned.

"Why not? I'm starving and I'm sure Sophie is too. Thanks Jess," Ned wiped the sweat from his brow.

Sophie grabbed the last seat, bringing the extra plates with her. "Jess will bring the other food and drinks over soon," she reported.

"Thank you," Hazel held herself in a way that screamed royalty. I'd noticed it before, and even here on the bench seat in the café, she held her back straight, hands poised in her lap. "Is there anything you can tell us about how the fire started?"

Sophie glanced at Ned. I saw him tilt his head forward, ever so slightly. She consulted her notepad. "Petrol was used as an accelerant.

Whatever the building contained is mostly burnt beyond recognition. The fire started in the doorway. It looks like the perpetrator, or perpetrators, doused everything and then stood outside and threw in a match." She flipped over to another page, "We've asked witnesses to the fire and no one can remember seeing anyone standing in the doorway or looking suspicious. Maybe they were distracted by the weird street parade or were just too busy to notice anything else going on."

I placed my glass of ginger beer carefully back on the table. "Over the last couple of days, I've seen Florence, Marigold, and Cindy and Mindy all enter that building," I left out the part about wanting to eavesdrop. "I thought it was odd, seeing as the building didn't appear to be in use. I've only lived here a few months, I thought maybe it's where the CWA or some other local group met." Did others in the village know it to be the meeting place for local community groups and not give it a second thought when they saw Florence and the others come and go from the building?

This time Ned spoke. "According to the council that building, and quite a few others around Misty Vale, are owned by a conglomerate of businesses based in the city." He patted his colleague on the arm, "Sophie is a whiz with technology. She's going to undertake a forensic interrogation of the documents available through the council records to confirm the details. I'm not a betting man, but I suspect we'll find the name Hartly all over this. Florence, her brothers-in-law, her daughters, and maybe some other local family names." He reached for the pitcher and poured himself a glass of the cooling fizzy drink.

"Would you mind keeping us up to date? If you could inform Jane of anything you discover, it would be greatly appreciated." I understood the hidden meaning behind my grandmother's words, playing matchmaker. While she'd picked up on my feelings, I remained thankful that this time my cheeks had not chosen to turn red. I focused on the piece of pizza on my plate and not at how closely I was sitting to the handsome policeman.

Another subtle nod of his head, though Sophie spoke first. "Does that mean you're going to step up into the leadership role? Is that the correct term?" She paused, referring to her notes, "I've only been here a couple of years, but I've read up on the history of the village."

Hazel drew herself up, her back straight, hands on the table in front of her this time. "With my granddaughter's help, and with the blessing of the village and the other founding family members, I'm willing to once again take the role in the village that I'm meant to, by virtue of my birthright. My intention is to train Clara, Jane, if she wants to be trained, to take on the role in the future." I wasn't particularly surprised, though we hadn't a chance to discuss that detail. I nodded my agreement.

Ned jotted a couple of words in his notepad, which he'd sat on the table next to his plate. "In that case, I'll liaise with you Jane. If it works for you, let's meet tomorrow, would midday here, for lunch suit you? That should give Sophie enough time to confirm what we think we know."

The café door jangled as two teenage girls ran in. "Ned, you'd better come see what's going on in the grotto!" Every pair of eyes in the café stared at the girls. Both dressed in blue jeans and green shirts, the teens worked at the local nursery after school, and on weekends. I recognised them but couldn't remember their names. They waited until Ned and Sophie were ready, then ran out, motioning for the officers to follow them. Everyone in the café, including Jess, followed. Hazel and I waited for the café to empty out, before we joined the crowd.

For the second time in a few hours, a crowd gathered at the front gate of the grotto. As more people joined, the noise was overwhelming. Everyone spoke loudly, competing to be heard, and gesturing at the antics inside the fence. It took me a couple of minutes to make sense of the scene in front of me.

A group of gingerbread men and snowmen were standing in a semicircle leaning over some much smaller toys made of wool, and wood.

The larger creatures were trying to intimidate the smaller ones, both groups were arguing, with raised voices, though with all the ruckus I couldn't make out specific words. The wooden soldiers weren't being much help. Their arms appeared glued to their sides. When they tried to nudge, rather than poke the offenders, the snowmen simply rocked back and forth, knocking the soldiers over like skittles. A herd of reindeer had managed to trample half of the side fence and were eating the vegetable garden in the yard next to the old school. A man and a woman, with short grey hair, jeans and worn shirts, stood a few metres away on their verandah, holding onto the railings, staring at the damage being done to their vegetables. Half a dozen elves in red, with tinsel wrapped around their hats, were climbing the gum trees that stood in the middle of the school yard. A platform laid across the branches a couple of metres into the tree, was laden with Christmas baubles. I watched in horror as the elves started throwing the colourful balls at the buildings. Most of the balls bounced off the walls, but the sound of breaking glass told me others hit their mark. So much for local elves not being as mischievous as their counterparts were known for.

Mindy, Cindy, and Nicholas were standing as close as they could without getting attacked by stray projectiles, videoing the scene, while Barabara was talking to camera. I couldn't hear her words, but with Florence beside her, I could imagine the lies that were being said.

Chapter Twenty-Nine

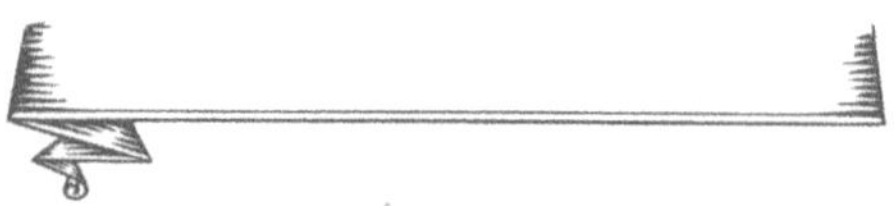

"Can we stop them broadcasting this?" I asked. Before Hazel could answer, two buses pulled into the street, parking at the end nearest the commotion. The faces peering out of the windows of the larger bus named, *The Wandering Nomads,* looked a little concerned at the escalating violence in the grotto. After a few seconds, the bus fired back to life, the driver manoeuvred the tightest u-turn I'd seen, before disappearing back the way it came. The sliding side door on the second, much smaller bus opened. The blonde sister, Cindy, hurried over and spoke to the man and woman who climbed out. The couple were probably mid to late twenties, dressed in black pants, the woman with a bright blue blouse, while the man sported a light pink shirt. Both carried recording equipment.

As Cindy began to lead them into the midst of the crowd, Ned and Sophie appeared and blocked their way. I didn't need to hear his words. Ned's frown and his finger pointed them back in the direction they came, left me in no doubt as to what he said. Cindy stood her ground, until Ned handed her his mobile. She listened to whoever was on the other end of the call. Each time she opened her mouth to speak, she closed it again. Finally, shaking her head, she handed the mobile back, and walked the newcomers back to their bus. As they drove away, she hurried back to her mother, her hands gesturing wildly as she whispered into her ear.

Barabara handed the microphone to Florence. "I think we need to move closer, so we can hear what's being said," I suggested. "Florence likely arranged the whole debacle and was about to blame someone else." Hazel nodded, and we moved closer to the gates surrounding the grotto. The crowd grew, as more curious residents came to investigate the commotion.

"This is what happens when magic goes wrong," Florence spoke firmly into the mouthpiece, whilst still managing to look serene. "Our village has been safe, a place where we can dabble in our magic, and not live in fear, until SHE arrived," Florence pointed her finger straight at where I was standing with my grandmother. "Hazel stepped down, went into hiding, then suddenly a woman turns up, pretending to be Hazel's granddaughter, and all THIS happens." With all the theatrics of an academy award winning actress, she turned and pointed with whole body arms at the scene playing out in the yard. More Christmas characters joined the snowmen's side, while additional toys had joined the others, creating a living pyramid of sorts, each side trying to outdo the other. "You can't seriously think that Hazel, and Jane, Clara, whatever her name is, have our villages best interests in mind. I've looked after this town and its residents for years. Choose me and I'll make sure we banish these...creatures," She waved in the direction of the schoolyard fight, "and all those responsible. The police haven't solved the thefts, break ins or the fire, and look – now we know why." She pointed to Ned, who'd made his way over to the gate and stood near Hazel and me.

The volume of the voices in the crowd rose as everyone shared their opinions. "I suspect this is just what Florence wants, to create such a feeling of panic, that everyone looks to her to resolve it," Hazel spoke tersely. Her lips pursed, making me thankful I wasn't on the receiving end of her wrath. I wanted to speak up, to defend Hazel, but if the crowd believed Florence, that I was an imposter, who'd believe me?

Cathy and Sophie waved as they manoeuvred through the crowd. Being in a police uniform didn't make their approach easier, with most of the people preoccupied with watching what the gingerbread men would do next. When they were close enough for Ned to hear them, Sophie said, "Ned, you need to listen to Cathy."

Ned moved his body a little so he could face Cathy and Sophie and keep an eye on the crowd. Hazel and I did the same. Normally calm, Cathy appeared flustered, her cheeks were flushed, and her neat hair looked as if something had pulled it out of place. "When the Christmas characters first appeared, I started some research, because I'm not from here I was curious how someone brings characters to life. During Halloween I assumed it was some kind of animation when the pumpkins rolled around town, broomsticks danced and the ghosts popped up, pretending to scare everyone. I learned the Kennys' could animate characters, but not on this scale. I spoke to Mrs Kenny earlier today. It's easy enough to learn to animate characters, if a fire and earth elemental team up. The same two people who created it, are the only two who can undo the spell."

"Florence is earth and Marigold is fire, and she may have been coerced to help," I mused. "There's definitely something wrong with Marigold, she's been acting strangely for a couple of days."

"I don't think it's Marigold, though someone could be influencing her to use her magic," Hazel spoke quietly. "Those daughters of Florence – didn't they attend some academy overseas? Their father's family were of questionable magic heritage."

"How do we make them undo the spell?" Cathy asked as a particularly noisy procession of wooden tractors and cars chased some smaller snowmen around the verandah on the old school building.

"If I could get the ruckus to pause for long enough, I could threaten them with gaol, where there are no mirrors, make up or social media, and all inmates wear an unflattering shade of grey," Ned lifted his cap and scratched the top of his head.

"I can help with the first part. I should be able to freeze all the animated creatures for a minute or two," Hazel said, a look of quiet determination crossed her face. "I used to be able to, though I may be a little out of practise."

"Can I help?" I asked. "I don't know how exactly, but as we are related, maybe," I hesitated, having no idea how I'd support when I'd no real experience in magic or enchantments. The children closest to the fence screamed in delight as the fire engine toys aimed their water hoses at the snowmen, spraying those nearest the gate with a wave of refreshing water. Even with the sun rapidly disappearing behind the horizon, the temperature was warm enough that to welcome the cold burst of liquid.

Hazel took hold of my hand. "You'll be able to tap into my energy and help me direct my power. We'll start with the characters, then the wooden toys and finally everything else. We'll keep them still as long as we can," she told Ned and Sophie. "When you are in position next to the girls, we'll make a start."

Ned and Sophie pushed through the crowd until they reached Cindy and Mindy, still filming, alongside Barbara and Nicholas. I couldn't hear specific words, but Barbara appeared in her element, directing Nicholas to film the police's approach.

As Ned tapped Mindy on the shoulder I felt my grandmother's energy, vibrating through my hand, up through my arm, until my body tingled with the power of our combined magic. I'd never experienced such a peaceful sensation. Rather than distracting me, the energy focused my concentration as I joined forces with my grandmother willing all the unnatural creatures and characters to cease movement.

Chapter Thirty

It felt like a lifetime, that we stood there, our power entwined, everything frozen in place, the crowd mesmerised. It also felt like it was over in an instant. As I came out of the trance, Cindy and Mindy were being handcuffed, Sophie and Ned flanking them to block any attempt at escape.

Beside me, Hazel shifted her weight from one foot to the other. "Are you okay?"

"Just a little weak, it's been a long time since I've used my power. I'll be fine in a minute."

In the grotto, the spell broken, the toys and Christmas characters, looked around, as if dazed, unsure of where they were. Slowly, the Christmas characters wandered into the main building, while the wooden and knitted toys headed for one of the smaller classrooms. A few elves remained in the tree but were no longer throwing colourful balls.

Surely the women would undo their enchantments rather than go to gaol? I wanted to lead my grandmother away, so she could sit down, but I didn't want to miss whatever was going to happen next. I settled for linking arms with her, so she could lean on me if she needed to.

"Someone needs to tell the crowd to go home, that the shows over, and there's nothing to worry about," my grandmother whispered.

I looked over to where Ned frowned, as he spoke to the two women in handcuffs. I didn't need to hear his words; his body language told me it wasn't going well. I patted my grandmother's arm and took a few steps forward. As I drew closer to the front of the gathering, I felt my skin warm on my cheeks as I swallowed the lump from my throat. "Excuse me everyone, some of you will know me as Jane. My other name is Clara, I'm Hazel's granddaughter. I know it's been a crazy few days here, but I want you to know everything is going to be fine." I pointed to the scene in the grotto, "This was created by those two women that Ned has in handcuffs. They've the power to un-animate the toys, and the Christmas characters, so that life can get back to normal in the village. They are choosing not to help. Their plan is to create a spectacle, to make our village into a tourist attraction. If we stay here and watch the drama, we're aiding them," I paused, realising the silence meant that everyone was listening to me. I glanced around the crowd. All eyes were focused on me. "I suggest we go back to whatever we were doing, before the shenanigans began."

"Who put you in charge?" Florence stepped in front of me, her feet slightly apart, hands on her hips, creating the illusion she was bigger and stronger than I. "What evidence do you have that you're Hazel's long-lost granddaughter? Why did you buy a cottage in the village under the name Jane Fairweather, if you are in fact Clara Thorne?"

I thought of and quickly disregarded the documents in the wooden box. Being in possession of the papers doesn't exactly prove my identity. Florence continued, without giving me the opportunity to defend myself. "How convenient that both Clara's parents have died, as have yours. Unless you're hiding another relative somewhere, or an employer who can vouch for you as Clara, you're an imposter who turned up here to take advantage of Hazel. The poor dear has suffered enough."

My blood boiled, as it raced around my body. Grey clouds appeared in the sky, which a few minutes ago had been clear. A strong gust of wind whooshed through the crowd, sending people ducking for cover. Before Hazel or I could defend our position against Florence's tirade, the hail started. I left Florence and hurried to my grandmother. As I grabbed her hand I guided her through the storm to her jeep.

Hazel let me drag her a few feet away from Florence, and the crowd before she dug her heels in. "You can stop now," she said calmly.

My body stopped, before my brain had a chance to register.

"If you run now, everyone will think Florence is right and you're an imposter. Let's go back to the café, have a coffee, or a hot chocolate. Let people see we've nothing to hide." Something in Hazel's tone broke through my panic, and drew me out of the flight mode, triggered by Florence's accusation.

As we arrived outside the café, with rain still pelting down. I took a few deep breaths in and out, thinking of Ned, stuck in the freak storm. What would happen when he realised that I was the culprit who created the weather event, by letting my emotions getting the better of me. He'd likely agree with Florence and want to run me out of town.

"Don't be ridiculous!" Hazel's voice penetrated my brain whirl. "I can teach you how to control your emotions. Ned's no fool. You don't have to prove who you are to me, or to him either. I can tell he likes you." With a wry smile at my expression of disbelief she added, "I can read people, not just their auras, but in some cases their thoughts."

As my dad's mother spoke, the wind died down. There were no longer giant raindrops pelting around us. The clouds flow along the sky, revealing the moon, half full, in the sky, surrounded by lots of twinkling tiny stars. I opened my mouth to speak, but no words came out. I closed my mouth. I let Hazel lead me inside, and find us a table, I was too preoccupied with the thoughts to focus on my surroundings.

"Jess is going to bring over some hot chocolate and some gingerbread," Hazel slid into the seat next to me. The café was quickly filling as other residents sought shelter from the freak storm. "You don't have to prove who you are to me," she patted me on the arm. "Does that happen a lot, bad weather when you are upset?"

"Yes, and not just weather, things break, electrical appliances burn out. I can control it, fifty percent of the time, if I catch my emotions in time." I felt my heart rate speed up, and I clenched my fists trying to stop whatever catastrophe would happen next.

Hazel's voice sounded firm, as if she was speaking to a small child, "You can absolutely control your magical outbursts. I can show you."

Whatever Hazel was about to say would have to wait, as Ned arrived at the table. "Do you mind if I join you?"

"You're welcome anytime," Hazel's words echoed my thoughts. "I didn't expect to see you so soon. Not that we're complaining." I nudged my grandmother under the table. She could read my thoughts, my feelings about the handsome man who was sitting so close to me. "What happened with the animated characters? Did Cindy and Mindy give in, with threat of gaol time?"

Ned frowned. I could tell he wasn't happy about the outcome, even before he filled in the details. "Cindy and Mindy have an uncle who is a lawyer. He made all sorts of threats to people above me, who strongly suggested I look elsewhere for the culprit," he tapped the table with his fingers. "I don't agree that we should give in to intimidation, I've asked Sophie to dig around and see if she can find evidence directing linking them to what's going on. If I'm wrong, I'll admit it, but I don't think I am."

At that moment Ned's mobile pinged. He glanced at the screen. "Oh! Really," he put his mobile on the table, "Look at this." We stared at the screen as Florence's face, blown up on a billboard stared back at us. The scene changed. Barbara held a microphone in front of Florence's smiling face. "In summary, I know the people of Misty Vale will do the right thing. We don't want to see those unnatural beings wandering around our precious haven. The police mistakenly thought my beautiful daughters caused the commotion, which is a horrible insult to the Hartly name. The Hartly's have always been here, protecting our village, when others chose to hide," She stared straight at the camera, with just the right mix of righteous indignation, compassion and determination. "Help me make sure our village is a place where we can all live together, without fear. Vote me in as mayor."

Chapter Thirty-One

The silence in the café was deafening. Most of the patrons had been watching the footage on their own assortment of mobiles, tablets, or laptops. I couldn't speak, and as I looked into Hazel's eyes, I saw the same mix of anger, frustration, and stubbornness I felt, deep in my soul. "How dare she!" I whispered. "I'm surprised she's not offering bribes to those who vote for her."

The reporter's face came on screen. "Why should the villagers vote for you?" Which was not an unreasonable question. I didn't disagree with a formal vote, but the timing was all wrong. Marigold mentioned the council, that the decision not to have a mayor had been made after careful consideration and discussion. Shouldn't the villagers have a say whether to nominate and vote in a mayor?

"That's an interesting question Barbara," Florence's words told me that question had been rehearsed. "Not that people should need an incentive for doing the right thing, but Cindy and Mindy are on board and willing to help any residents who want to, to set up their own small business in the village. It's our way of giving back to the community."

I resisted the urge to throw my chair back in disgust. If I walked outside right now, there was no guarantee I wouldn't say something I would regret. Or worse, cause a tidal wave, or an avalanche. I took in a deep breath, held it for a few seconds, and exhaled. I repeated the steps until the urge to hit someone passed. As Barbara's face appeared back in shot, wrapping up the interview, I turned away. My energy bouncing around my body gave me an idea. I turned to Hazel, aware that Ned was watching me. "I have a question about our family. Why are we meant to lead and look after the village? It has something to do with our powers, doesn't it?" Hazel's eyes stared back into mine; she didn't nod but I felt I was onto something. "We can undo any magic that's created, if the result is not in the best interests of the residents. Our powers will counteract any spells or enchantments that are created for the wrong reasons." Once again, I picked up on the unspoken signal that I was on the right track. "And as I have a double dose of spirit power, so to speak, because of the ancestry of my parents. That probably means I possess an unique blend of magic." Turning towards the police officer, I added, "I could probably get rid of the occupants of the grotto. I'm only just figuring out what abilities I have and what I can do. I generally ignore that side of myself."

"I see, well that explains a lot," Ned replied. I wasn't sure what he meant, and I didn't get a chance to ask as Jess approached our table with a tray laden with goodies.

"Misty Vale residents are quite accepting and open minded, but this is going too far," Jess unloaded three mugs of hot chocolate and a plate piled high with gingerbread cookies on to our table. Pointing to Ned's mobile, still lying on the table, she added, "I thought even Florence would have the courtesy to wait for the town meeting tomorrow."

"It is disappointing," Hazel agreed. "I know I'm the last one to comment on how a residents behaviour impacts the town, but first she organises to sell out our families for the sake of money and notoriety, then she uses a significant amount of money to buy votes."

The bell jangled as more customers entered the café. "We're all able to make our own choices. Those who are greedy and dishonest would do so whether you'd stepped down or not," Jess said gently. "You walked away, but we all have the responsibility to look after ourselves and our town. When the council considered all options they decided on a caretaker role, which is why we don't have a mayor, and why Misty Vale residents aren't exiled if they're found to be using their magic for less than noble reasons. Florence mightn't be on council, but she influences those who are, leading from the sidelines, in the role you vacated. She's played the long game, slowly coercing people with money and power to bend to her will." She patted Hazel on the arm, as she left, returning to the counter where customers were lining up.

I saw a sadness in Hazel's eyes, they glistened as the tears welled. "Are you okay?" Before she could answer, I added. "Jess is right. We all have free choice. If not Florence, someone else would have acted badly, greedily, looking to make money from their power. In the last five years, there's been an increased interest in all things magic and witch related, in the world in general. The pandemic stirred that sense of looking for otherworldly solutions."

Hazel's mouth quivered as she attempted a smile, "That's true. Misty Vale is lucky to have been spared the limelight for so long. Now it's about minimising collateral damage."

I eyed the pile of gingerbread and added a cookie to the plate in front of me. "I'm right by your side; whatever you want to do. Try not to worry. I read people too, though I haven't put a lot of effort into honing the skill. Still, it appeared to me that although those in the crowd were cautious, most would welcome you back," I touched her hand slightly. "Now if you don't mind, I'm going to eat my cookie and drink my hot chocolate."

"Best idea ever," my grandmother agreed, as a small smile played on her lips.

Ned picked up his mug and a couple of cookies. "If you don't mind, I'll leave you to it. I need to meet Sophie, write up the days incidents and explain to our bosses why we arrested the Hartly sisters," he tucked his chair under the table as he stood. "I'll text you tomorrow Jane and we'll catch each other up on anything to note. I suspect, after seeing the interview, that there will be more incidents." Ned smiled as he shook Hazel's hand, "It's so good to see you out again Hazel. It's been too long.

I was only a baby when...but my parents and their friends speak highly of you, how much you loved and protected our village."

As Ned left the café, my thoughts drifted, to a scene where Ned and I were sharing an intimate dinner for two. *Not that it's going to happen, while I can't control my powers, nor can I prove who I am.* I absent mindedly played with the ring, still on my finger, where I'd slid it after finding it in my box of treasures. I pulled it a little to test it, but it still wouldn't budge.

"Where did you get that?" Hazel asked, pointing to the ring. The coloured gems glistened brightly in the café lighting.

"I found it in a box I'd been carrying around since I left home. It must have been mums, but I don't remember seeing it before. When I slipped it on to see how it looked, it got stuck. I haven't been able to take it off. It's funny, I forgot all about it until just now. I swear it wasn't glistening during the day."

"May I?" Hazel held out her hand. I laid mine on top of hers, so she could inspect the ring more closely. "I suspect this may be the item that will prove your heritage. The Devlin ring, an heirloom passed down through the women of the Devlin family. There's a book in the library with a picture of it." My heart skipped at her words. Maybe I could prove who I was after all.

"Would you like to meet at the library tomorrow morning, before the town meeting?" I asked, drinking the last of my drink. "Sorry, but I'm suddenly exhausted and I need to go home. My animals will be wondering where I am."

"Of course. Would you like me to drive you?" I heard the concern in my grandmother's voice.

"Thanks, but the fresh air will do me good," I gave Hazel a huge hug. "Thank you, for being here for me, for being my family. For believing I'm your family."

She squeezed me tightly. As she let go, she reminded me, "Seeing as I am the one who found you, who sought you out, of course I believe in you."

Hazel and I left the café together, waving at Jess as we did. I was tempted to walk Hazel to her jeep, where we'd left it behind the row of shops. "I'll be fine, granddaughter of mine. Be careful walking home, stay to the lit areas," with those words, she disappeared down the laneway that led to the carpark.

The moonlight shadows danced along in front of me, lighting my way home. The streetlights helped too. Walking at night never scared me. There was something magical about walking in semi-darkness, imagining creatures lurking behind every tree.

The two cars, that slowly drove past me, rounded the block and crawled past for a second time, made my skin crawl. I put my head down, to quell the nausea in the pit of my belly and walked as fast as I could back to my cottage.

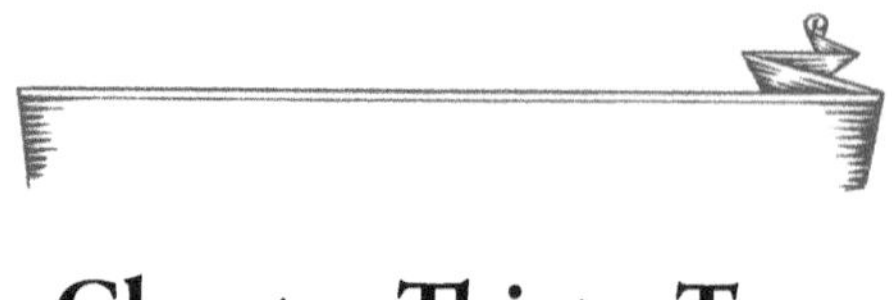

Chapter Thirty-Two

The pounding on my door woke me. "Hang on, I'm coming," I called as I navigated the bundles of fur who raced ahead of me to see who was knocking at our door at such an early hour in the morning.

Finding Ned on my doorstep I was thankful I'd fallen asleep in old leggings and a t-shirt, while watching Christmas movies, trying to calm myself after the events of the day. "Hi Jane. Did I wake you? I didn't mean to," Ned sounded odd, not his usual upbeat, positive self. Maybe he'd had a sleepless night too.

"No...I mean yes...I'm normally awake by now so don't stress. Would you like a cuppa?" I wished I'd brushed my hair or at least retied it into a responsible ponytail before opening the door.

"I'm afraid I can't, although I'd love to," the police officer looked uncomfortable, as if ants were biting his feet, he was fidgeting, as he stood on the doorstep. "I'm here, officially, to ask if you have any way of proving who you are? That you are Jane, or Clara...Hazel's grand-daughter? I've had a formal complaint asking me to investigate you, your identity," his cheeks reddened. Ned looked like he was about to burst into tears. "I've seen those documents that you found in the box under the coffee table. As none of the documents included your photo-graph, they don't exactly prove your identity."

My head pounded. I really needed a coffee if I was going to think straight. Sprinkles and Cinnamon were jumping and prowling in front of me. "Oh, for goodness sake, just come in would you, please. One cof-fee won't hurt, and if I don't feed these two, let's just say there's a whole level of berserk with a hungry pup that we don't want this early in the morning," I left Ned with the choice to either follow me or stand at the door. I needed caffeine.

To his credit, Ned sat at the table quietly, after filling the kettle with water, while I followed the morning routine with Bert, Sprinkles and Cinnamon. I decided I liked the policeman enough that I'd be mortified if he arrested me. An image flashed in my brain, of our first date being interrupted by my arrest for being a wicked witch. I suppressed a chuckle, lest Ned thought I'd lost the plot.

After the animals were safely out in the backyard for their morning dose of sun, and two mugs of coffee sat on the kitchen table, I spoke, "You do remember that the wooden box found me, I didn't come to town saying I was Clara Thorne. I didn't know about Clara Thorne until I read the documents left under my coffee table. Would a family heirloom that can be traced back to my mother's family, the Devlin's, be enough evidence of who I am?"

"I know that the box of information found you. What type of family heirloom are we talking about? I was hoping that maybe you had photos of yourself with your parents, growing up. We should be able to see a family resemblance. That way Florence and the other villagers who went to school with your parents could identify them," Ned suggested. "You make the best coffee," he added after drinking nearly half of his mug in one go.

I smiled, "Thanks. That would be a good idea, except I didn't take any photos with me when I left home...unless..." I sprang to my feet, only just catching my chair before it toppled to the floor. I heard Ned's footsteps behind me as I rummaged in the tallboy, removing the cardboard box from where I'd mistakenly placed it into the wrong drawer. The little book about the bear who travelled with his little red suitcase, was just the sort of place I'd have tucked a photo in, or if I was lucky, where my parents would have tucked away some sort of evidence or proof of my true identity. "Oh, my goodness," as I turned to the last page in the little book I noticed an envelope, tucked into the cover, hidden in a way that I only saw it because I was actively seeking to find something. Gently, I removed the envelope from the old hardbound cover, replacing the book in the box, ensuring the lid fitted tightly in place.

I lifted the flap of the faded cream colour envelope, one that belonged to a good quality stationery set, back when writing thank you letters was something done for every gift received. Inside were two photographs. The first a muted colour square photograph, from one of the instamatic cameras of the 1960's. It showed my parents, much younger than I remembered them, with a baby in their arms. The second picture – of the day I graduated high school, my parents and I were easily recognisable. As if placed there by magic, or by my parents in answer to my pleas. Without a word, I passed the photographs and the envelope to Ned.

"That's good enough for me, as long as someone other than Hazel, can vouch that your parents are in fact from Misty Vale," he tucked the photographs into the envelope and passed it back to me.

I refused to take the envelope. "Keep it, show whoever you need to. I only ask that you keep them yourself. Please don't hand them to Florence, Marigold, even Sophie," the familiar sting of hot, salty tears welled in my eyes. I blinked them away.

Ned gently touched my arm, just for a second. Did he have the same warm, tingling sensation, starting in his fingertips, shooting up his arms to the back of his neck, that I did? I didn't want the moment to end.

"What's that?" Ned asked, pointing to the gemstone ring on my finger.

As I opened my mouth to reply, I noticed the gems were glowing, "The family heirloom I mentioned, the Devlin ring, which I didn't know about until Hazel noticed it yesterday. I found it in the same box as the photographs, my parents must have put it in there when I left home, though I'd not noticed it until a few days ago." My skin around the ring tingled. The red ruby and the purple amethyst shone a little brighter than the others, making me wonder if the crystals had different properties, or correspondences, as I'd heard them called. "I'm meeting Hazel at the library before the town meeting, to verify this ring, apparently it's documented in a book on the Devlin family."

"Can I borrow it, to verify with one of the Devlin's?"

"You could, but it won't come off," I demonstrated by tugging at the ring, which glowed even more brightly, but didn't budge one iota.

"May I?" I nodded as Ned moved closer and tried to gently coax the ring off my finger. The gems shone even more brightly, as the gap between us shrunk. I heard my heart beating, or was it his? I sat mesmerised by his closeness. The touch of his skin on mine sent sweet tingles shooting around my body.

We jumped apart, as the beeping of Ned's mobile startled us both. "I've got to take this," he said apologetically. "I'll see you at the meeting."

Standing at the front door, I watched Ned, as he hopped into his car, still talking on his phone. I could still feel his touch, and the electric energy that filled the gap between us when we stood close. The ruby twinkled, confirming my thoughts. I couldn't wait to spend more time with the local police officer.

Chapter Thirty-Three

It took no time at all, to get ready for the day. My stomach refused to settle, a herd of butterflies making any attempt at breakfast futile. I settled for peppermint tea, in a bid to calm my nerves.

By 8am I could stand it no longer. "You lot, behave, I love you, and I'll be back as soon as I can," I bade my family goodbye, made sure my windows and doors were locked, and left the safety of my cottage.

"I see the family resemblance now."

"Margot, hi, I didn't see you there." Could she hear my heart pounding in my chest, as I steadied myself on the gate post, taking care to avoid getting a splinter in my palm.

"You're Clara, aren't you? I knew your mother, and you look a lot like her, not that I've seen her since we were teenagers. Oh, we used to get up to mischief," she said wistfully. "We were cousins, you see, and friends."

"I'd love to hear some of those stories, my parents didn't talk about their past at all."

"Another day, dear, we can have a good old chat over a cuppa, or a gin," she grinned. "Your mother's favourite drink back in the day." She rose to her feet, holding on to a shovel rammed into the ground as she did so. I resisted the urge to jump in and help her, remembering her independence. "Are you going to help Hazel challenge that evil woman? She must be stopped, and you're clearly who you say you are," she pointed to my hand. "You're wearing the Devlin ring, even Florence can't deny that."

I moved my hand, watching as all the gems sparkled in the daylight. My breathing evened as I contemplated the piece of jewellery I wore. "You don't happen to know any details about this by any chance?" If she knew my parents, she may be able to provide useful information, ahead of today's meeting.

"Most of what I knew once I've forgotten, unless it has to do with plants," she waved her arms, encompassing her garden, the greenhouse and the vegetables and fruit trees I could glimpse beyond the house. "I do recall that Devlins and Thornes were both spirit elementals, which is why there was such a kerfuffle when you parents got together," Her eyes glazed over wistfully as she cast her mind back thirty odd years. "Something about balance, control, insight, and power...but don't quote me on that."

"I won't," I smiled. "Thank you, for telling me what you remember. I'm going to the library with Hazel, to find more information before the village meeting. Have a good day." I left Margot to her plants, smiling as I heard her singing to them as she finished weeding around her roses.

Mr Quin was in his garden, with his back to the footpath. I didn't call out a greeting lest I startled him. He wasn't steady on his feet, and he was busy pruning a wisteria vine hanging off his verandah.

I wish I knew more about elemental powers and how the ring worked. The green stone caught my eye, distracting my train of thought. As I recalled Ned's touch, a warm feeling spread through my body. This time the ruby glowed brighter. *I wonder.* I pictured Hazel, watching my finger as the blue stone shone. *Could the ring be attuned to my power somehow?*

"Jane Fairweather," There was no kindness in Florence's tone.

"Florence Hartly," I returned the greeting, gritting my teeth as I spoke. My fists automatically forming fists. I concentrated on unclenching them slowly. The village didn't need a freak storm on this warm sunny morning.

"What are you up to?" The matriarch sneered, making her question sound more like an accusation.

I took in a breath and exhaled slowly, maintaining eye contact with the woman as she moved to block my way. "That's none of your business," I kept my tone even and made a move to step to one side to pass her.

Florence pre-empted my move and stepped to prevent me. "I'm concerned for the safety of our village." The ground beneath us shuddered. As an earth elemental could she command the earth to open and swallow me?

I wasn't about to find out if I was being too dramatic. "And I'm happy to contact the police and ask them to make sure you stay away from me." The yellow stone on my hand sent a bolt of electricity out towards the feet of the woman who blocked my way.

She stood her ground. "Are you trying to hurt me?" she screeched. I heard the surprise in her voice. "Not that it matters, as you can't prove who you are, I'll be requesting that you are removed from Misty Vale and not allowed to return."

My blood pounded in my temples. I started to clench my fists but loosened my grip as my ring replied for me, letting loose more sparks at the edge of her open toed sandals.

Hazel approached from behind Florence. I shoved my detractor a little as I pushed passed her and enveloped my grandmother in a hug. "There you are!" My grandmother smiled, "I wanted to show you the most adorable Christmas patterned material." I linked my arm in Hazel's as she led me into *The Crafty Owl*.

Once we were safely inside, I whispered, "Thank you. I didn't want Florence to know where we were headed. She's already spoken to Ned and is planning to run me out of town." I hugged my grandmother.

"Hazel, Jane, two of my favourite crafters," Cathy beamed as she walked out from the wool aisle.

"Good morning, Cathy," my grandmother and I replied in unison.

"We're here to check out some of your Christmas materials. We have errands to run so if we can leave our purchases here and pick up later, that would be awesome," Hazel continued.

"Of course! Pick out what you'd like, and I'll have them cut to size and folded before your return," she responded.

Ten minutes later we'd picked out some fabrics, worked out the sizes we required and paid for our purchases. I was excited to make some table runners and tablecloths. Sewing wasn't one of my favourite crafts, but the tiny characters on the fabric were so cute.

Chapter Thirty-Four

"The hide of that woman!" Hazel said indignantly when I provided details about Ned's visit and running into Florence. "I've a good mind to give her a piece of my mind," she huffed.

"While I'm ever so grateful you want to defend me, that'll be giving her exactly what she wants. Let's use evidence and logic. The photographs, the documents, and this ring, should be enough to prove my heritage."

"You never noticed the photographs, or the ring in your keepsake box, until now?" Hazel mused. "Your parents used a powerful cloaking spell, or you simply brought them into existence because you needed them. Knowing how much your parents wanted to leave Misty Vale behind, I'd suggest it was the latter," she considered her next words. "Part of the reason behind forbidding liaisons between families with specific elemental magic, came from fear. We didn't know whether any offspring would have stronger powers, lacking in powers, or what long term repercussions might be."

"Am I the only person to be born of a union between two such families?" I asked as we entered the library. I waved a hello to Kelly. She sat on the mat in the children's area, in front of a group of toddlers.

"Not now, you were the first, from Misty Vale, to be born of two families with a similar magic. At least, the first one we were aware of. Too late, we came to the painful conclusion that children from such unions had the same chances as any other children." Tears filled my grandmother's eyes, the stones in my ring sparkled, even in the muted lighting of the reading room.

I touched her arm, the stones sparkling brightly as we connected. "We can't change the past. Let's make sure Misty Vale has a positive future." I led her to the books I'd found on the history of the village.

Hazel read the spines on the history books. Extracting one from the shelf she took it to the nearest table. I slid into the seat next to her, marvelling at the craftmanship of the wooden furniture in the reading room, as she flicked through the pages. She passed the book to me. "The furniture in the library was created by a particularly talented class of students, at least fifty years ago."

Wondering if I'd get used to Hazel reading my mind, I read the pages of the open book. A brief history of my great grandfather the jewellery maker, and the magical ring he fashioned. The ring disappeared years ago. "How could I have made the photographs and the ring manifest into the box I'd carried with me for years? I've no idea how to do that. This ring is old, and magical, and not a figment of my imagination."

"The problem is, you're trying to apply logic to a situation that's infused with magic. It's not about intellect or understanding. Hidden deep within you, without any formal training, is a power that's stronger than most others in the village. Contained within, you also possess the knowledge you need, to master your powers." Hazel scanned the shelf in front of us, where the history of Misty Vale was set out in old dusty editions. "Let's try something simple. One of these books recounts how Misty Vale came to be the home of the millet broom. Don't look with your eyes, find it with your third eye, your intuition."

As Hazel spoke, in my mind I saw a thinnish book, with a brown cover. A paperback with a picture of a sweeping broom on the front. I heard a thud, as a skinny book, the size I pictured, fell backwards out of the shelf onto the vinyl floor.

I gasped.

My grandmother smiled but said nothing. The book I retrieved was exactly as I pictured it. "Let's try something else," she said. "What colour pen have I got my handbag?"

"Green," I answered almost immediately as an image of a green pen popped into my mind. "Green ink and a green coloured outside casing as well."

Hazel rummaged around in her bag, and pulled out a writing implement identical to the picture in my head. "Before you ask, I don't have different coloured pens hiding in my bag."

"You can read minds, I wish I could do that," It was clear I still didn't understand the magnitude of the gifts I possessed.

You can read minds. I heard my grandmother's voice, but I didn't see her lips move. *Focus on Kelly, at the counter. What is she thinking about?*

I frowned at my grandmother, still not sure, but I did as she asked. "She's wondering if she left the iron on at home, and whether she should go home and check. Oh, and she thinks the new barman at the pub is cute and wants to ask him out," I felt my cheeks heat at the thoughts I'd invaded. "Have I always been able to do that? If so, why haven't I noticed?"

"Because you never tried," Hazel turned to face the doors. "Who will come into the library next?"

Beginning to enjoy the game, the first image in my head was Ned, in uniform. My cheeks returned to their rosy hue, as they often did when I thought of my new friend. "Well, that can't be right," I muttered. I tried again, and still Ned appeared in my mind.

"Never dismiss your intuition," was Hazel's response, as she pointed to Ned, entering the library.

"Hazel, Jane, I'm glad I caught you before you headed to the meeting. Florence has bought forward the meeting time. It starts in a few minutes," Ned sounded out of breath, as if he'd jogged to pass on that information.

"Thanks for telling us Ned," Hazel spoke before I could find my voice. "It's lucky I know a shortcut," she continued as she took each of our hands in hers. "Close your eyes, or you may feel dizzy." A second later I heard Hazel's voice again, "You can open your eyes now."

We were standing at the back of a church hall. I noted the weathered wooden floor, worn walls with years of scuff marks and dents in them, and the skinny metal window frames. Around a hundred residents were seated in the portable chairs, placed neatly in rows in front of the little stage. A dais, complete with a microphone sat on the stage. More residents milled around the well-stocked coffee, tea, and biscuits table along the side wall. Hazel and I responded to nods of acknowledgement, while Ned, after briefly touching my shoulder in a show of support, made his way to the front of the room.

Florence, her daughters, and the annoying reporter were setting up on the stage. I looked to Hazel. She nodded at the question I'd not yet asked. I led her along the side of the hall, until we joined Ned and the others at the centre of the stage.

"Before you start throwing defamatory remarks around," Ned was saying to Florence, "Jane has proven her identity and several locals have confirmed she is in fact Clara Throne, daughter of Sandra Devlin and Alexander Thorne, and granddaughter of Hazel Thorne."

My knees wobbled, as if their bones had turned to jelly. I channelled my energy around my body until it connected with the piece of jewellery on my finger. The emerald and topaz sparkled, confirming...what...that I was finally learning to control my powers?

Florence's face grew redder than the dresses worn by her daughters.

"Who's acting as mediator?" Ned continued, as Florence tried to edge away from him.

"I am," Barbara shoved the microphone in Ned's face.

Rather than step back from the recording device, the police officer spoke into it, "Just make sure you're fair when running it, or I'll shut down the meeting quicker than you can say action."

Barbara turned towards the crowd, those seated and the late comers standing at the back of the room, "Misty Vale needs someone who is going to look out for the best interests of the village and its residents. Are you going to vote for Florence, whose family has been instrumental in ensuring the safety and wellbeing of everyone for nearly forty years, or Hazel and the newcomer?"

The room exploded in an uproar. I heard snippets, as people voiced their opinions, "The Hartly's are crooks...you nincompoop, they're the best thing that's happened to our village...Hazel for mayor...how do we know Jane is who she says she is...did you see the ring she's wearing...the Devlin ring...it disappeared...vote for Florence...her daughters are good lookers..."

"Enough!" The lights in the hall flickered. It took a few seconds for me to realise I'd spoken. "Everyone can have their say, but let's do it in a way we can all hear and comment. Put your hand up if you have something to say, and Barabra will pop over with her microphone, so we all hear you." I waited, to see what would happen next. A ripple of subdued murmuring ran through the crowd. After a few more seconds, the voices died down. A few hands tentatively rose in the air. Barabra looked at Florence, who shrugged, trying not to frown at me. I felt more in control than at any other time in my life.

The reporter held the microphone in front of an older lady, about Florence's age. "My name's Penelope. Florence helps the village with so many charities, she's helped us raise lots of money and she always knows who's available to help."

An older man, I recognised as a friend of Mr Quin's raised his hand. "Florence's husband was a crook, so are his brothers. I don't trust anything her daughters say."

A younger woman nursing a baby raised her hand. "I heard those two talking about creating a conference centre and tourist attraction in town. We bought our home here because it's a quiet, safe place to bring up our children. We'll move if it becomes a tourist destination."

Marigold rose her hand, "I don't like how Hazel stepped down and ignored everything...before...but Jane asks a lot of questions and seems to have a positive energy." Florence glared and took a step towards her friend, until Ned stepped in front of her.

"Let's give Hazel and her granddaughter a chance," I recognised the woman who spoke as Jess's mother. A few people nodded and mumbled their support.

"This is ridiculous!" Florence spoke loudly, ensuring her voice carried to the back of the room. "We don't all need a say. You just need to let me keep doing what I'm doing. I've spoken to many of you about the benefits of letting Hartly Enterprises find the right businesses to grow our village. We've a few companies ready to break ground in a week or so. As part of the revamp of the village, if you are keen to promote or establish your own business, talk to my daughters and they'll provide any assistance you need. It's as simple as that." The ground under the building moved, as Florence's elemental magic ran along the floor and out under the building, grounding itself. Barbara, who was hurrying back to Florence, tripped over her own high heeled shoes.

Chapter Thirty-Five

Voices in the crowd escalated, as people digested the latest information, that some big corporation was about to invade the village. "Let's all sit down, quietly," Florence said loudly. "Cindy and Mindy will hand around slips of paper and pencils. Just write down your preference for mayor and you can all go back to whatever you had planned for the day."

Sophie entered through the side door, making a beeline for Ned. She handed him a piece of paper, whispering in his ear.

"Hold on!" He commanded in a voice that left me in no doubt he expected to be obeyed. "I asked Sophie to undertake a deep dive into both families," I saw him inhale, exhaling a few seconds later as he held up a piece of paper. "Florence and her brothers-in-law have been the subject of a criminal investigation. This document proves they've been embezzling money from a variety of sources, for years. Cindy and Mindy's role in the theft and deception has been confirmed." As he spoke, a couple of police offers in uniform entered and handcuffed the three Hartly women. After a futile attempt at fighting, Florence and her daughters allowed themselves to be led out of the building.

Slowly, people in the crowd started to talk amongst themselves. "You said you had information on both families?" Called out a voice from the back of the room. A man I recognised as the owner of the newsagents stood up. I couldn't recall his surname, or if he was affiliated with any particular local family.

"Jane Fairweather grew up not knowing who she was. In a box she's been carrying around for years, she found a ring, that has been confirmed to be the Devlin family heirloom, and photographs of herself with her parents. I've asked some of the people who went to school with Sandra and Alexander, and they've confirmed the identity of the people in the photograph." He hoisted himself up onto the stage. "Look, I don't know whether my opinion means anything here, but I don't think you need to make any decision today. Hazel and Jane...Clara...will look out for us, with or without any of us making a formal decision."

I read the room, many of the residents looked like they had questions. I plonked myself next to Ned. "Ask me anything, and I'll answer to the best of my ability." Hazel caught my eye, nodding imperceptibly toward the reporter. She was right, no one would be comfortable speaking up in front of Barabara and Nicholas. "Barbara, Nicholas, will you please leave. You can pack up your equipment once we are finished in here." I waited until Nicholas dragged Barbara out the side door. "Okay, so does anyone have any questions? Nothing you say will be recorded. This is a safe space. Also, I don't need to tell you, but you're all free to leave at any time." My proximity to Ned, made it a little difficult to think straight. I figured I'd wing any answers, but it looked like no one was keen to start the ball rolling.

"As far as I'm concerned, I trust Hazel, and if you're her granddaughter, I trust you too." A woman I didn't recognise stood up. "I like Florence, but she wasn't the right person." A few people got up and shuffled out the back doors, whether in response to what was said, I couldn't be sure.

"I don't know if I trust you or not, but I'm willing see how things pan out. I mean, our village is pretty good at looking after itself." A man I'd seen at the hardware store shrugged as he stood to leave.

Cathy stood up. "May I make a suggestion?" I watched as most of the people in the room turned to face her. "I love this village, though

I've only been here a few years. I'd hate to think someone like Florence, or anyone, is able to change our village, without getting agreement from the majority of our residents. If we were to choose set up a council, with a mayor, clear policies and guidelines, it would help guarantee the safety of the village."

"I agree," Hazel faced the people who remained in the hall. "Let's take our time and work it out properly. We don't need to jump into anything right now. Why don't we meet back here in a few days."

After everyone left the hall, I helped Penelope, and the others pack the chairs away. "It's good to have you home," Penelope said as I helped her pile the chairs into the tiny room to the side of the main room. "You look so much like your mother; I went to school with her for a while," she said softly. "Your father, I remember, as a leader, class captain for a couple of years."

"I wish I'd known about their lives here. At least now I understand why I feel such an affinity with this village." Suddenly I knew what I had to do. "Thank you, Penelope, I hope I see you again soon." I made my way back to where Ned and Hazel were packing away the coffee and tea. "Are the creatures still creating havoc in the village?"

"The last report I received was yes, the snowmen were chasing some knitted toys around the park, and the gingerbread men were riding the reindeer up and down the main street." Images of the unnatural characters and the trouble they were causing popped into my head as Ned spoke. I tried not to giggle.

"I think it's about time we fixed that problem," I led them out through the doors and across the street to the grotto. "Do I have to see them all, or have them all in the one place to get rid of them?" I asked aloud. As I looked into Hazel's eyes, we both knew I'd figured out the answer. I took a few steps away from Ned and Hazel, I didn't want anything to happen to them if my magic backfired. I held my hands by my side, stretching my fingers out wide, allowing my energy to flow through my body. I focused my energy, joining with the earth, the ground, the air, fire, water and remnants of the spirit, left behind by whoever had created the characters. The gems on my finger gleamed and glistened in the sunlight. I focused on my energy linking to the elements of the earth, air, fire, water, and spirit. I drew power from around me, through my body and out through the ring in search of every creature that shouldn't be alive. One by one I felt the characters disappear, into nothingness. As if they never existed. I stood in the same position until I felt the shift in the air around me.

As if waking from a trance I re-entered reality, where Hazel and Ned stood by watching me. "Is it done?" Ned asked.

"I think so."

The clock that stood above the library chimed eleven times. As my eyes adjusted to the sunlight, the street appeared a little quieter than normal. As if the craziness of the last few days had calmed down. A subtle difference in the atmosphere.

"Balance restored." My grandmother confirmed.

Ned raised his hand. "I'm not sure I understand what just happened here, but may I buy both you ladies a cuppa, and one of Jess's scrumptious Christmas cupcakes?"

My heart did somersaults in my chest as I linked arms with my family and my friend.

Home.

The End

Sarah Lewin

If you want to know more about me or my books, here are some details. Alternatively, please make contact via any of the social media listed below:

Email: sarahlewin@sarahlewin.com.au

You Tube: https://youtube.com/@sarahlewinangelwisdom539

Blog: https://sarahlewin.com

Facebook: https://www.facebook.com/SarahLewinAuthorWitchyMysteryBooks

Instagram: https://www.instagram.com/sarahlewin_author/

Amazon: https://amazon.com/author/sarahlewin

Goodreads: https://www.goodreads.com/author/show/43342156.Sarah_Lewin

Book Bub: https://www.bookbub.com/authors/sarah-lewin

My Witchy Mystery Books:

<u>Witch Wisdom Series:</u>

#1 – *Crone Wisdom*

#2 – *Ancient Wisdom*

#3 – *The Wisdom of the Witches*

There are two free novellas in this series

The Coven

Kai's Story

<u>Spirit Town Cozy Mysteries:</u>

#1 – *Autumn Leaves Are Falling*

#2 – *Secrets Ghosts and Whispers*

#3 – *The Ghosts of Spirit Town*

<u>Misty Vale Cozy Mysteries:</u>

#1 – *A Very Crafty Christmas*

<u>I also have a range of children's books available, and some more cozy mysteries due for release in 2025.</u>